PUFFIN BOOKS

Once.

Morris Gleitzman grew up in England and went to live in Australia when he was sixteen. He worked as a frozen-chicken thawer, sugar-mill rolling-stock unhooker, fashion-industry trainee, department-store Santa, TV producer, newspaper columnist and screenwriter. Then he had a wonderful experience. He wrote a novel for young people. Now he's one of the bestselling children's authors in Australia. He lives in Melbourne, but visits Britain regularly. His many books include *Two Weeks with the Queen*, *Water Wings*, *Bumface*, *Boy Overboard* and *Toad Rage*.

Visit Morris at his website:
www.morrisgleitzman.com

Once.

MORRIS GLEITZMAN

PUFFIN

PUFFIN BOOKS

Published by the Penguin Group
Penguin Books Ltd, 80 Strand, London WC2R 0RL, England
Penguin Group (USA) Inc., 375 Hudson Street, New York, New York 10014, USA
Penguin Group (Canada), 90 Eglinton Avenue East, Suite 700, Toronto, Ontario, Canada M4P 2Y3
(a division of Pearson Penguin Canada Inc.)
Penguin Ireland, 25 St Stephen's Green, Dublin 2, Ireland (a division of Penguin Books Ltd)
Penguin Group (Australia), 250 Camberwell Road, Camberwell, Victoria 3124, Australia
(a division of Pearson Australia Group Pty Ltd)
Penguin Books India Pvt Ltd, 11 Community Centre, Panchsheel Park, New Delhi – 110 017, India
Penguin Group (NZ), 67 Apollo Drive, Rosedale, North Shore 0632, New Zealand
(a division of Pearson New Zealand Ltd)
Penguin Books (South Africa) (Pty) Ltd, 24 Sturdee Avenue, Rosebank, Johannesburg 2196, South Africa

Penguin Books Ltd, Registered Offices: 80 Strand, London WC2R 0RL, England

puffinbooks.com

First published in Australia by Penguin Group (Australia),
a division of Pearson Australia Group Pty Ltd 2005
First published in Great Britain in Puffin Books 2006
This edition published 2009
2

Text copyright © Creative Input Pty Ltd, 2005
All rights reserved

The moral right of the author has been asserted

Set in 13/15pt Minion
Made and printed in England by Clays Ltd, St Ives plc

British Library Cataloguing in Publication Data
A CIP catalogue record for this book is available from the British Library

ISBN-13: 978–0–141–32988–8

www.greenpenguin.co.uk

Penguin Books is committed to a sustainable future
for our business, our readers and our planet.
The book in your hands is made from paper
certified by the Forest Stewardship Council.

For all the children
whose stories have never been told

Once I was living in an orphanage in the mountains and I shouldn't have been and I almost caused a riot.

It was because of the carrot.

You know how when a nun serves you very hot soup from a big metal pot and she makes you lean in close so she doesn't drip and the steam from the pot makes your glasses go all misty and you can't wipe them because you're holding your dinner bowl and the fog doesn't clear even when you pray to God, Jesus, the Virgin Mary, the Pope and Adolf Hitler?

That's happening to me.

Somehow I find my way towards my table. I use my ears for navigation.

Dodie who always sits next to me is a loud slurper because of his crooked teeth. I hold my bowl above my head so other kids can't pinch my soup while I'm fogged up and I use Dodie's slurping noises to guide me in.

I feel for the edge of the table and put my bowl down and wipe my glasses.

That's when I see the carrot.

It's floating in my soup, huge among the flecks of cabbage and the tiny blobs of pork fat and the few lonely lentils and the bits of grey plaster from the kitchen ceiling.

A whole carrot.

I can't believe it. Three years and eight months I've been in this orphanage and I haven't had a whole carrot in my dinner bowl once. Neither has anyone else. Even the nuns don't get whole carrots, and they get bigger servings than us kids because they need the extra energy for being holy.

We can't grow vegetables up here in the mountains. Not even if we pray a lot. It's because of the frosts. So if a whole carrot turns up in this place, first it gets admired, then it gets chopped into enough pieces so that sixty-two kids, eleven nuns and one priest can all have a bit.

I stare at the carrot.

At this moment I'm probably the only kid in Poland with a whole carrot in his dinner bowl. For a few seconds I think it's a miracle. Except it can't be because miracles only happened in ancient times and this is 1942.

Then I realise what the carrot means and I have to sit down quick before my legs give way.

I can't believe it.

At last. Thank you God, Jesus, Mary, the Pope

2

and Adolf Hitler, I've waited so long for this.

It's a sign.

This carrot is a sign from Mum and Dad. They've sent my favourite vegetable to let me know their problems are finally over. To let me know that after three long years and eight long months things are finally improving for Jewish booksellers. To let me know they're coming to take me home.

Yes.

Dizzy with excitement, I stick my fingers into the soup and grab the carrot.

Luckily the other kids are concentrating on their own dinners, spooning their soup up hungrily and peering into their bowls in case there's a speck of meat there, or a speck of rat poo.

I have to move fast.

If the others see my carrot there'll be a jealousy riot.

This is an orphanage. Everyone here is meant to have dead parents. If the other kids find out mine aren't dead, they'll get really upset and the nuns here could be in trouble with the Catholic head office in Warsaw for breaking the rules.

'Felix Saint Stanislaus.'

I almost drop the carrot. It's Mother Minka's voice, booming at me from the high table.

Everyone looks up.

'Don't fiddle with your food, Felix,' says Mother Minka. 'If you've found an insect in your bowl, just eat it and be grateful.'

The other kids are all staring at me. Some are grinning. Others are frowning and wondering what's going on. I try not to look like a kid who's just slipped a carrot into his pocket. I'm so happy I don't care that my fingers are stinging from the hot soup.

Mum and Dad are coming at last.

They must be down in the village. They must have sent the carrot up here with Father Ludwik to surprise me.

When everyone has gone back to eating, I give Mother Minka a grateful smile. It was good of her to make a joke to draw attention away from my carrot.

There were two reasons Mum and Dad chose this orphanage, because it was the closest and because of Mother Minka's goodness. When they were bringing me here, they told me how in all the years Mother Minka was a customer of their bookshop, back before things got difficult for Jewish booksellers, she never once criticised a single book.

Mother Minka doesn't see my smile, she's too busy glaring at the Saint Kazimierz table, so I give Sister Elwira a grateful smile too. Sister Elwira doesn't notice either because she's too busy serving the last few kids and being sympathetic to a girl who's crying about the amount of ceiling plaster in her soup.

They're so kind, these nuns. I'll miss them when Mum and Dad take me home and I stop being Catholic and go back to being Jewish.

'Don't you want that?' says a voice next to me.

Dodie is staring at my bowl. His is empty. He's sucking his teeth and I can see he's hoping my soup is up for grabs.

Over his shoulder, Marek and Telek are sneering.

'Grow up, Dodek,' says Marek, but in his eyes there's a flicker of hope that he might get some too.

Part of me wants to give my soup to Dodie because his mum and dad died of sickness when he was three. But these are hard times and food is scarce and even when your tummy's stuffed with joy you still have to force it down.

I force it down.

Dodie grins. He knew I'd want it. The idea that I wouldn't is so crazy it makes us both chuckle.

Then I stop. I'll have to say goodbye to everyone here soon. That makes me feel sad. And when the other kids see Mum and Dad are alive, they'll know I haven't been truthful with them. That makes me feel even sadder.

I tell myself not to be silly. It's not like they're my friends, not really. You can't have friends when you're leading a secret life. With friends you might get too relaxed and blurt stuff out and then they'll know you've just been telling them a story.

But Dodie feels like my friend.

While I finish my soup I try to think of a good thing I can do for him. Something to show him I'm glad I know him. Something to make his life here a bit better after I've gone, after I'm back in my own home with my own books and my own mum and dad.

I know exactly what I can do for Dodie.

Now's the moment. The bath selection has just started.

Mother Minka is standing at the front, checking Jozef all over for dirt. He's shivering. We're all shivering. This bathroom is freezing, even now in summer. Probably because it's so big and below ground level. In ancient times, when this convent was first built, this bathroom was probably used for ice skating.

Mother Minka flicks her tassel towards the dormitory. Jozef grabs his clothes and hurries away, relieved.

'Lucky pig,' shivers Dodie.

I step out of the queue and go up to Mother Minka.

'Excuse me, Mother,' I say.

She doesn't seem to notice me. She's peering hard at Borys, who's got half the playing field under his fingernails and toenails. And a fair bit of it in his armpits. I can see Mother Minka is about to flick her tassel towards the bath.

Oh no, I'm almost too late.

Then Mother Minka turns to me.

'What is it?' she says.

'Please, Mother,' I say hurriedly. 'Can Dodek be first in the bath?'

The boys behind me in the queue start muttering. I don't glance back at Dodie. I know he'll understand what I'm trying to do.

'Why?' says Mother Minka.

I step closer. This is between me and Mother Minka.

'You know how Dodek's parents died of sickness,' I say. 'Well Dodek's decided he wants to be a doctor and devote his life to wiping out sickness all over the world. The thing is, as a future doctor he's got to get used to being really hygenic and washing himself in really hot and clean water.'

I hold my breath and hope Dodie didn't hear me. He actually wants to be a pig-slaughterer and I'm worried he might say something.

Mother Minka looks at me.

'Get to the back of the queue,' she says.

'He really needs to be first in the bath every week,' I say. 'As a doctor.'

'Now,' booms Mother Minka.

I don't argue. You don't with Mother Minka. Nuns can have good hearts and still be violent.

As I pass Dodie he gives me a grateful look. I give him an apologetic one. I know he wouldn't mind about the doctor story. He likes my stories. Plus I think he'd be a good doctor. Once, after he pulled the legs off a fly, he managed to stick a couple back on.

Ow, this stone floor is really cold on bare feet.

That's something Dodie could do in the future. Design bathroom heating systems. I bet by the year 2000 every bathroom in the world will be heated. Floors and everything. With robots to pick the twigs and grit out of the bathwater.

Look at that, Borys is the first one in and the water's brown already. I can imagine what it'll be like when I finally get in. Cold, with more solid bits in it than our soup.

I close my eyes and think about the baths Mum and Dad used to give me. In front of the fire with clean water and lots of warm wet cuddles and lots and lots of stories.

I can't wait to have a bath like that again.

Hurry up, Mum and Dad.

Once I stayed awake all night, waiting for Mum and Dad to arrive.

They didn't.

They haven't.

But it's alright. Nobody drives up that narrow rocky road from the village in the dark unless they're Father Ludwik. He says God helps him and his horse with the steering.

Mum and Dad were never very religious so they probably wouldn't risk it.

They'll be here once it's daylight.

What I'm worrying about now is whether they'll recognise me after three years and eight months.

You know how when you have a haircut or a tooth comes out, your parents carry on about how you must be the kid who belongs to the shoe mender down the street?

Well I've changed even more than that. When I arrived at this place I was plump and little with freckles and two gaps. Now I'm about twice as tall with glasses and a complete set of teeth.

I press my face against the cold windowpane over my bed and watch the sky start to go pale and tell myself not to be silly. I remind myself what Mum and Dad said when they brought me here.

'We won't forget you,' Mum whispered through her tears. I knew exactly what she was saying. That they wouldn't forget to come and get me once they'd fixed up their bookshop troubles.

'We'll never forget you,' Dad said in a husky voice, and I knew exactly what he was saying too. That when they come, even if I've changed a lot, they'll still know it's me.

The sun is peeping up behind the convent gates. Now it's getting light outside I don't feel so anxious.

Plus, if all else fails, I've got my notebook.

The cover's a bit stained from when I had to snatch it away from Marek and Borys in class. It was to stop them reading it and some ink got spilled, but apart from that it looks exactly like it did when Mum and Dad gave it to me. It's the only notebook with a yellow cardboard cover in this whole place, so they'll definitely recognise it if I hold it in an obvious way when they arrive.

And when they read it, they'll know I'm their son because it's full of stories I've written about them. About their travels all over Poland discovering why their bookshop supplies suddenly went so unreliable. Dad wrestling a wild boar that's been eating authors. Mum rescuing a book printer who's been kidnapped by pirates. Her and Dad crossing the border into Germany and finding huge piles of really good books propping up wobbly tables.

Alright, most of the stories are a bit exaggerated, but they'll still recognise themselves and know I'm their son.

What's that sound?

It's a car or truck, one of those ones that don't need a horse because they've got an engine. It's chugging up the hill. I can hear it getting closer.

There go Sister Elwira and Sister Grazyna across the courtyard to open the gates.

Mum and Dad, you're here at last.

I'm so excited I'm steaming up the window and my glasses. I rub them both with my pyjama sleeve.

A car rumbles into the courtyard.

Mum and Dad must have swapped it for the old bookshop cart. Trust them, they've always been modern. They were the first booksellers in the whole district to have a ladder in their shop.

I can hardly breathe.

Half the dormitory are out of bed now, pressing their noses against the windows too. Any second now they'll all see Mum and Dad.

Suddenly I don't care if everyone does know my secret. Perhaps it'll give some of the other kids hope that the authorities might have made a mistake and that their mums and dads might not be dead after all.

That's strange. The car windows are steamed up so I can't see clearly, but it looks like there are more than two people in the car. Mum and Dad must have given Father Ludwik a lift. And a couple of his relatives who fancied a day out.

I can't make out which ones are Mum and Dad.

I hold my notebook up for them to see.

The car doors open and the people get out.

I stare, numb with disappointment.

It's not Mum and Dad, it's just a bunch of men in suits with armbands.

'Felix,' says Dodie urgently, grabbing me as I hurry out of the dormitory. 'I need your help.'

I give him a pleading look. Can't he see I'm doing something urgent too? Finding out from Mother Minka if Mum and Dad sent a note with the carrot saying exactly when they'll be arriving. I've got the carrot with me to jog Mother Minka's memory.

'It's Jankiel,' says Dodie. 'He's hiding in the toilet.'

I sigh. Jankiel's only been here two weeks and he's still very nervous of strangers.

'Tell him there's nothing to worry about,' I say to Dodie. 'The men in the car are probably just officials from Catholic head office. They've probably just come to check that all our parents are dead. They'll be gone soon.'

12

I give a careless shrug so Dodie won't see how nervous I am about the officials. And how much I'm desperately hoping Mother Minka remembers the story we agreed on about my parents. About how they were killed in a farming accident. Tragically.

'Jankiel's not hiding from the men in the car,' says Dodie. 'He's hiding from the torture squad.'

Dodie points. Marek, Telek, Adok and Borys are crowding into the dormitory toilets.

'Come on,' says Dodie. 'We've got to save him.'

Dodie's right. We can't leave Jankiel at the mercy of the torture squad. Marek and the others have been after him since the day he arrived. He's their first new boy to torture in three years and eight months.

Since me.

Dodie shoves the toilet door open. We go in. Marek, Telek, Adok and Borys have got Jankiel on his knees. Jankiel is pleading with them. His voice is echoing a bit because they've got his head half in the toilet hole.

'Don't struggle,' says Telek to Jankiel. 'This won't hurt.'

Telek's wrong. It will hurt. It hurt when they did it to me three years and eight months ago. Having your head pushed down a toilet hole always hurts.

'Wait,' I yell.

The torture squad turn and look at me.

I know that what I say next will either save Jankiel or it won't. Desperately I try to think of something good.

'A horse crushed his parents,' I say.

Now the new kid is staring at me too.

I grip my notebook hard and let my imagination take over.

'A great big plough horse,' I continue. 'It had a heart attack in the mud and fell onto both his parents and it was too heavy for him to drag off them so he had to nurse them both for a whole day and a whole night while the life was slowly crushed out of them. And do you know what their dying words to their only son were?'

I can see the torture squad haven't got a clue.

Neither does the new kid.

'They asked him to pray for them every day,' I say. 'At the exact time they died.'

I wait for the chapel bell to finish striking seven.

'At seven o'clock in the morning,' I say.

Everyone takes this in. The torture squad look uncertain. But they're not pushing anybody down the toilet, which is good.

'That's just one of your stories,' sneers Telek, but I can tell he's not so sure.

'Quick,' says Dodie. 'I can hear Mother Minka coming.'

That's a story too because Mother Minka is down in the courtyard with the head office officials. But Marek and the others look even more uncertain. They swap glances, then hurry out of the toilets.

Dodie turns wearily to Jankiel.

'What did we tell you?' says Dodie. 'About not coming in here on your own?'

Jankiel opens his mouth to reply, then closes it again. Instead he peers past us, trying to see down into the courtyard.

'Have they gone?' he says.

Dodie nods and points towards the dormitory.

'Borys is putting mud in your bed,' he says.

'I mean the men in the car,' says Jankiel.

He looks almost as scared now as he did with the torture squad.

'They'll be gone soon,' I say. 'Mother Minka's dealing with them.'

Jankiel starts to look a bit less nervous, but only a bit. I find myself wondering if he's got secret alive parents too.

'Thanks for saving me,' he says. 'That was a good story about my parents being crushed.'

'Sorry if it brought back sad memories,' I say.

'Nah,' says Jankiel. 'My parents froze to death.'

I stare at him. If that's true, it's terrible. Their bath must have been outdoors or something.

Jankiel glances down at my notebook.

'Do you make up lots of stories?' he asks.

'Sometimes,' I say.

'I'm not very good at stories,' he says.

As we go out into the dormitory I find myself wondering if Jankiel is Jewish. He's got dark eyes like me. But I don't ask him. If he is, he wouldn't admit it. Not here.

Dodie stays with Jankiel, who's peering nervously out the window again, and I head off, hoping that Mother Minka has got rid of the officials so I can ask her about Mum and Dad.

As I hurry down the stairs I glance out the window myself.

In the courtyard Mother Minka is having an argument with the men. She's waving her arms, which she only does when she's in a very bossy mood.

I stop and stare.

What's that smoke?

It's a bonfire. The men are having a bonfire in the courtyard. Why are they doing that? It can't be for warmth, the sun's up now and it's going to be a hot day.

I can see why Mother Minka's so angry. The smoke is going into the chapel and the classrooms and the girls' dormitory.

Oh no, I've just seen what the men are burning.

That's terrible.

If Mum and Dad saw this, they'd be in tears.

The other nuns are down there in the courtyard, and some of them have got their faces in their hands.

I'm feeling very upset myself.

The men are burning books.

Once I saw a customer, years ago, damaging books in Mum and Dad's shop. Tearing pages out. Screwing them up. Shouting things I couldn't understand.

Mum was crying. Dad was furious. So was I. When customers are unhappy they should ask for a refund, not go mental.

These men are just as bad. They're hurting books cruelly and viciously and laughing about it.

Why?

Just because Mother Minka is a bit bossy? That's no reason to destroy the things she loves most in the world except God, Jesus, the Virgin Mary, the Pope and Adolf Hitler.

Wait a minute, those wooden boxes the men are flinging around are book boxes from our library.

I get it.

Mother Minka was complaining to us library monitors only last week that the library was very messy and needed a tidy-up. She must have got sick of waiting for us to do it and called in professional librarians in professional librarian armbands. They've reorganised the library and now they're burning the books that are left over.

No wonder Mother Minka is so upset. I bet she didn't give them permission to do that.

Me and Mum and Dad would have taken those books. We love all books, even old and tatty ones.

I can't watch any more.

I turn away from the smoke and flames and hurry down to Mother Minka's office. Rather than risk mentioning Mum and Dad out there, I'll wait for her to come back inside.

I stand by her desk.

Suddenly a voice yells at me. It's not Mother Minka, it's a man's voice, and he's shouting in a foreign language.

I turn, trembling.

In the doorway stands one of the librarians. He's glaring at me very angrily.

'This isn't a library book,' I say, pointing to my notebook. 'It's my notebook.'

The librarian scowls and takes a step towards me.

I'm confused. Why would Mother Minka call in foreign librarians? Perhaps people who don't speak Polish are faster library tidiers because they don't get tempted to read the books before they tidy them.

Mother Minka hurries into the room. She looks very unhappy. I'm starting to think this isn't a good time to ask her about Mum and Dad.

'What are you doing here?' she demands.

I can't tell her the truth in front of the librarian, so I try to tell her that I've come down to make sure none of the sparks from the fire blow in and singe her furniture or stationery. But at this moment, with her and the librarian glaring at me, I can't get the words out.

'Um . . .' I say.

'I remember now, Felek,' says Mother Minka. 'I asked you to come down and collect your notebook. Now you've got it, go back upstairs.'

I stare at her, confused.

Why is she calling me Felek? My name's Felix.

I don't wait to try and work it out. I head for the door. The librarian is still scowling at me. Mother Minka is still looking very stern. But also, I see as I brush past her, very worried.

Suddenly she grabs my ear.

'I'll take you myself,' she says.

She drags me along the corridor, but instead of dragging me upstairs, she pulls the kitchen door open and bundles me inside.

I've only been in the kitchen a few times before, to trim mould off bread as a punishment for talking in class, and I'd forgotten what a great soupy smell there is in here.

I don't have a chance to enjoy it today.

Mother Minka has shut the door behind us and is crouching down so her face is level with mine. She's never done that before, ever.

Why is she acting so strangely?

Maybe whoever trimmed her bread for dinner last night didn't do a very good job. Dodie says eating bread mould can affect your brain.

'This must be terrible for you,' she says. 'I wish you hadn't seen what they're doing out there. I didn't think those brutes would bother coming all the way up here, but it seems they go everywhere sooner or later.'

'Librarians?' I say, confused.

'Nazis,' says Mother Minka. 'How they knew I had Jewish books here I've no idea. But don't worry. They don't suspect you're Jewish.'

I stare at her.

These Nazis or whatever they're called are going around burning Jewish books?

Suddenly I feel a stab of fear for Mum and Dad.

'When my parents sent the carrot,' I say, 'did they mention when they'd actually be getting here?'

Mother Minka looks at me sadly for a long time. Poor thing. Forgetting my name was bad enough. Now she's forgotten what Mum and Dad told her as well.

'Felix,' she says, 'your parents didn't send the carrot.'

I desperately try to see signs of bread-mould madness in her eyes. It must be that. Mother Minka wouldn't lie because if she did she'd have to confess it to Father Ludwik.

'Sister Elwira put the carrot in your soup,' says Mother Minka. 'She did it because she . . . well, the truth is she felt sorry for you.'

Suddenly I feel like I'm the one with bread-mould madness burning inside me.

'That's not true,' I shout. 'My mum and dad sent that carrot as a sign.'

Mother Minka doesn't get angry, or violent. She just puts her big hand gently on my arm.

'No, Felix,' she says. 'They didn't.'

Panic is swamping me. I try to pull my arm away. She holds it tight.

'Try and be brave,' she says.

I can't be brave. All I can think about is one awful thing.

Mum and Dad aren't coming.

'We can only pray,' says Mother Minka. 'We can only trust that God and Jesus and the Blessed Mary and our holy father in Rome will keep everyone safe.'

I can hardly breathe.

Suddenly I realise this is even worse than I thought.

'And Adolf Hitler?' I whisper. 'Father Ludwik says Adolf Hitler keeps us safe too.'

Mother Minka doesn't answer, just presses her lips together and closes her eyes. I'm glad she does because it means she can't see what I'm thinking.

21

There's a gang of thugs going round the country burning Jewish books. Mum and Dad, wherever in Europe they are, probably don't even know their books are in danger.

I have to try and find Mum and Dad and tell them what's going on.

But first I must get to the shop and hide the books.

Dodie opens his eyes wide even though we're kneeling in chapel and meant to be praying.

'Jewish?' he says. 'You?'

I nod.

'What's Jewish?' he says.

It's too risky to try and explain all the history and geography of it. I've already spent most of this prayer telling Dodie about Mum and Dad and why I have to leave. Father Ludwik has just turned round and he's got eyes like that saint with the really good eyesight.

'Jewish is like Catholic only different,' I whisper.

Dodie thinks about this. He gives me a sad look.

'I'll miss you,' he whispers.

'Same here,' I say.

I give him the carrot. It's fluffy and a bit squashed, but I want him to have it because he hasn't got a mum and dad to give him one.

Dodie can't believe it.

'Is this a whole carrot?' he says.

'When I come back to visit,' I say, 'I'll bring more. And turnips.'

I wait till everyone's gone into breakfast, then I creep up to the dormitory to pack.

I pull my suitcase from under my bed and empty it out. The clothes I was wearing when I arrived here are much too small for me now, so I stuff them back into the suitcase and slide it back under the bed. Best to travel light.

All that's left are the books I brought from home and the letters Mum and Dad wrote to me before the postal service started to have problems.

I put the books on Dodie's bed. They're my favourite books in the whole world, the William books by Richmal Crompton that Mum and Dad used to read to me. William was their favourite when they were kids too, even though Richmal Crompton isn't a Jewish writer, she's English. I used to think Mum and Dad were translating the words into Polish themselves, but then I found out somebody had already done it.

I've always loved the William stories. He always tries to do good things, and no matter how much mess and damage he causes, no matter how naughty he ends up being, his mum and dad never leave him.

Dodie knows I'd never give these books away for ever. When he finds them on his bed he'll know I'll be back for a visit.

I pick up my notebook, tear out a clean page and write a note.

Dear Mother Minka,
Thank you very much for having me. Please don't worry, I'll be fine. If possible, can Dodie have my soup?
Yours faithfully,
Felix

I put my notebook and pencil and letters inside my shirt.

I'm ready.

I peer out the window. The sun is shining brightly. The Nazis have gone. The courtyard is empty except for a pile of smoking ash and a few charred books.

If I'm quick, I can be out of here before everyone finishes breakfast.

I hurry past the other beds, trying not to feel sad about going, and I'm just about to leave the dorm when somebody steps in through the door and blocks my way.

Jankiel.

'Don't go,' he says.

I stare at him, my thoughts racing. He must have overheard me telling Dodie about leaving. I remember him asking me about making up stories. He must want me to stay and teach him how to make up stories himself.

I can see he's desperate, the poor kid. Desperate for something to keep the torture squad's mind off stuffing him down the toilet.

'You know how to make up stories already,' I say.

'What?' he says.

'Stories,' I say. 'Half of Saint Jadwiga dorm's still blubbing over that story you told them while we were queuing for chapel. About all the different ways you tried to get the dead horse off your parents. Cranes. Tugboats. Balloons. That was brilliant. Some of those girls were looking at you in that weepy adoring way nuns look at Jesus.'

'Really?' says Jankiel, sounding pleased.

'Here,' I say, pulling out my notebook. 'Here's what a story looks like written down. Practise as much as you can and you'll be fine.'

I tear out a page for him. It's the story where Mum and Dad hack their way through the jungle to a remote African village and help mend some bookshelves.

'Thanks,' says Jankiel.

He looks so confused and grateful I know he won't mind if I excuse myself and hurry off.

I'm wrong. As I move past him he suddenly looks desperate again and grabs my arm.

Oh no. If I try and fight him to get away and he starts yelling, every nun for a hundred miles around will come running.

'Don't go,' he says. 'It's too dangerous.'

I know what he means. If the nuns see me

sneaking out I'll be history, but I've got to risk it.

I pull myself out of Jankiel's grip.

'There are Nazis everywhere,' he says.

'I know,' I say. 'That's why I have to go.'

Jankiel screws up his face and stares at the floor.

'Look,' he says, 'I can't tell you what the Nazis are doing because Mother Minka made me swear on the Bible that I wouldn't tell anyone. She doesn't want everyone upset and worried.'

'Thanks,' I say. 'But I know what they're doing. They're burning books.'

Jankiel looks like he's having a huge struggle inside himself. Finally he gives a big sigh and his shoulders slump.

'Just don't go,' he says. 'You'll regret it if you do. Really regret it.'

For the first time I feel a jab of fear.

I squash it.

'Thanks for the warning,' I say. 'That vivid imagination of yours is going to be really helpful when you need to make up more stories.'

He doesn't say anything. He can see I'm going.

I go.

Once I escaped from an orphanage in the mountains and I didn't have to do any of the things you do in escape stories.

Dig a tunnel.

Disguise myself as a priest.

Make a rope from nun robes knotted together.

I just walked out through the main gate.

I slither down the mountainside through the cool green forest, feeling very grateful to God, Jesus, the Virgin Mary, the Pope and Adolf Hitler. Grateful that after the Nazis left this morning, the nuns didn't lock the gate. Grateful that this mountainside is covered in pine needles rather than tangled undergrowth and thorns.

Mother Minka took us out on an excursion once, to look for blackberries. Dodie got tangled in thorns. He cried for his mum, but she wasn't there.

Only me.

Stop it.

Stop feeling sad about him.

People who feel sad make careless mistakes and get caught. They trip over tree roots and slide down mountains on their heads and break their glasses and the nuns hear them swearing.

I slither to a halt and listen carefully, trying to hear if Father Ludwik and his horse are on the mountain road looking for me.

All I can hear is birds and insects and the trickle of a stream.

I push my glasses more firmly onto my face.

Mum and Dad are the ones who need me now.

I think about getting to the shop and hiding our books and finding a train ticket receipt which tells me where Mum and Dad are and which train I have to catch to find them.

I think about how wonderful it'll be when we're all together again.

I have a drink from the stream, and head down the mountain through beams of golden sunlight.

You know how when you haven't had a cake for three years and eight months and you see a cake shop and you start tasting the cakes even before they're in your mouth? Soft boiled buns oozing with icing. Sticky pastries dripping with chocolate and bursting with cream. Jam tarts.

I'm doing that now.

I can smell the almond biscuits too, even though I'm crouching in a pigpen and there's a very smelly pig sticking its snout in my ear.

Over there, across that field, is Father Ludwik's village. It must be, it was the only village I could see as I was coming down into the valley. One of those buildings must definitely be a cake shop. But I can't go any closer, not wearing these orphanage clothes. Father Ludwik has probably put the word around that an escaped orphan is on the loose. Plus Nazi book burners could be in the general store buying matches.

The pig is looking at me with sad droopy eyes.

I know how it feels.

'Cheer up,' I say to the pig. 'I don't want to waste time in that village anyway.'

I need to get to my home town. And the good news is I know it's on a river that flows near here. When Mum and Dad drove me to the orphanage in the bookshop cart, we travelled next to the river almost the whole way to the mountains.

The pig cheers up.

It snuffles the sore patches on my feet.

'You're right,' I say. 'These orphanage shoes hurt a lot. I need to get some proper shoes from somewhere, ones that aren't made from wood, and some proper clothes, and directions to the river.'

The pig frowns and I can see it's trying to remember where the river is.

It can't.

'Thanks for trying,' I say.

Thinking about cakes has made me hungry. I

didn't have breakfast this morning and now it's past lunchtime.

I look wistfully at the pig's food. It's grey and lumpy like Sister Elwira's porridge. My mouth waters, but there's not enough in the rusty trough for both of us. I can see the pig is happy to share, but I don't feel I should. The pig is stuck here and this is all it's got.

I'm lucky. I can get food anywhere. I'm free.

Thank you God, Jesus, Mary, the Pope and Adolf Hitler for answering my prayers.

A house.

I'm sorry I started doubting you while I was lost in the fields. And blaming you for the scorching sun and lack of puddles to drink.

This is perfect. A house on a deserted road without any nosy neighbours or police stations close by. And on the wall next to the front door is one of those carved metal things that religious Jewish families in our town have on their houses.

I knock.

The door swings open.

'Hello,' I call. 'Anyone at home?'

Silence.

I call again, louder.

Still no reply.

I wish I had Mother Minka with me for advice about what to do next, but I don't and I'm desperately thirsty, so I go into the house, hoping the owners aren't deaf and unfriendly.

If they are, it doesn't matter, because they're not here. All three rooms in the place are empty. The people must have left in a big hurry because there are two half-eaten meals on the kitchen table and one of their chairs has fallen over.

I pause, listening carefully.

What's happened? Where are the people?

I pick the chair up.

The kitchen stove is still burning and the back door is wide open.

I stick my head out. The garden and the fields next to it are all empty.

In the distance I hear faint gunshots.

Of course. That explains it. They're out hunting. They must have seen some rabbits, grabbed their guns and gone after them in a big hurry.

They probably won't be back for ages. When Father Ludwik goes rabbit hunting he's usually gone for hours.

On the kitchen table is a jug of water. I drink most of it. Then I eat some of the potato stew on each plate. I leave a bit in case the people are hungry when they get back.

In one of the other rooms are some clothes and shoes. None of them are for a kid, but I guess you can't have all your prayers answered in one day.

I take off my orphanage clothes, put on a man's shirt and trousers, trim the ends off the arms and legs with a kitchen knife, and use the bits of cloth to wedge around my feet in a pair of man's shoes.

Then, while my clogs and orphanage clothes are burning in the kitchen stove, I tear a page from the back of my notebook and write a note.

Dear People Who Live Here,
Sorry. I know stealing is wrong but I haven't got any money. And my mum and dad's books are in great danger. I hope you understand.
Yours faithfully,
Felix

I can't find a single map in the house, but it doesn't matter. I think I know which way the river is now. In the distance I can hear more gunshots. Dad read me a hunting story once, about how deer and foxes and rabbits prefer to live near lakes and rivers. So the hunters from this house are probably over near the river.

Thanks, Dad.

I eat one more mouthful of the potato stew and cut a piece off a loaf of bread and put it inside my shirt with my notebook and letters. I find a hat and put it on and clean my glasses and lace up the shoes as tightly as I can.

Then I set off along the road towards the gunshots.

This is just like a story I wrote once.

The two heroes (Mum and Dad) come to a

lonely crossroads. They're not sure which way to go to get to their destination (the cave of a troll who wants to buy a full set of encyclopedias). So they use their ears for navigation. They listen carefully until, in the distance, they hear the troll noisily eating farm animals, and that tells them they have to turn left.

I'm doing the same standing here at these crossroads. I'm listening really hard. But I'm having trouble hearing any more gunshots because here it's the countryside that's noisy. Birds chirping in the trees. Insects chattering in the sunshine. Fields of wheat rustling in the breeze.

Sometimes real life can be a bit different to stories.

I adjust my hat, which keeps slipping down over my ears.

Wait a second.

Over there.

Gunshots.

Thank you God and the others.

I head along a road that's wider than the last one. This one's got wheel tracks in the dust. Not the usual smooth cartwheel tracks with hoof marks between them. These are the jagged tracks of rubber truck tyres.

I hope a truck comes along soon because now that I'm wearing ordinary clothes and I don't look like a runaway orphanage kid, I can ask for a ride.

A horse cart would be fine too.

Anything to get me to the river and our town and our books more quickly.

At last, a truck.

I stand in the middle of the road and wave my hat.

As the truck gets closer I see it's a farm animal truck packed with people. They're standing in the back, squashed together.

That's strange, they don't look like they've got many clothes on. Why would half-naked people be packed into a truck like that?

I get it, they must be farm workers going on holiday. They're so excited about having a swim in the river that they've undressed already. I don't blame them, this sun's really hot.

I'm still waving but the truck isn't slowing down. It's speeding up, driving straight at me.

'Stop!' I yell.

The truck doesn't stop.

I fling myself off the road into the long grass. The truck speeds past, spraying me with dust and grit and engine fumes.

I can't believe it. That truck driver was so busy daydreaming about his holiday, he didn't even see me.

Wait a minute, there's another one coming. This one's painted in brown and grey splotches. I think it's an army truck.

This time I wave from the side of the road, just in case.

'Hey,' I yell. 'Can I have a ride?'

There are soldiers sitting in the back. Some of them see me and point. One raises his rifle and pretends to aim at me.

That's very nice of him, giving a country kid a thrill, but I'm not a country kid, I'm a town kid and I need to get home urgently.

'Please,' I yell.

This truck doesn't slow down either. As it passes it hits a hole in the road and all the soldiers bounce up into the air.

Suddenly there's a loud bang.

I fall back into the long grass.

I'm stunned with shock. I've been shot at. The soldier shot at me. The bullet whizzed so close to my head I can still hear it buzzing in my ear.

I roll over and lie as flat as I can in case any of the other soldiers have a go.

None of them does. I start to breathe again. It must have been an accident. The bounce of the truck must have made the gun go off.

I have another thought.

That poor soldier. Tonight in the barracks he'll hardly be able to swallow his dinner he'll be so upset. All he wanted to do was play a little trick and now he thinks he's shot an innocent kid.

I scramble to my feet and wave at the truck, which is disappearing down the road.

'Don't worry,' I yell. 'I'm alright.'

But the truck has vanished into the dust cloud

from the first truck, so the soldier doesn't see me and they don't give me a ride.

What bad luck.

For me and him.

At last, the river.

After walking such a long way, it's so good to kneel on the cool stones, stick my face in the water and have a drink.

This river is beautiful. The water is gleaming gold in the sunset, and the warm air smells damp and fresh, and there are millions of tiny insects turning happy floating cartwheels in the soft light.

Last time I was here, when I was six, I must have been too young to notice how beautiful Poland is in summer. Though there is another reason why I love this river so much now.

It's going to lead me home.

I stand up and look around.

The little road beside the river is still here, just like I remember it. The road that goes all the way to our place. Shame it's too narrow for trucks, but you can't have everything.

I'm feeling really good now, even though I'm a bit hungry because I'm trying to make my bread last and one mouthful wasn't a very big dinner.

I've still got a lot more walking to do, but in my heart I feel like I'm almost home. And I don't feel so anxious about the Nazi book burners because I've worked out what they're doing. They're burning books in the villages and remote orphanages first, before winter comes, so they don't get cut off by the snow. Which means they probably haven't done any of the towns yet, so I'll be in plenty of time to hide our books.

What's that noise?

Boy, gunfire's loud when it's so close. That lot startled me so much I almost fell into the water. The hunters must be just round that bend in the river.

Another burst of gunfire, a long one.

And another.

Sunset must be when loads of rabbits come out. Or perhaps the hunters are just using up their bullets to save carrying them home.

I'm glad I'm not going in that direction. I'm glad I have to head this way, the same way the river's flowing, away from the mountains.

Look at that. The river has suddenly turned red. Which is a bit strange, because the sunset is still yellow.

The water's so red it almost looks like blood. But even with all those gunshots, the hunters couldn't have killed that many rabbits.

Could they?

No, it must just be a trick of the light.

Once I walked all night and all the next day except for a short sleep in a forest and all night again and then I was home.

In our town.

In our street.

It's just like I remember. Well almost. The street is narrow like I remember and the buildings are all two levels high and made of stone and bricks with slate roofs like I remember, but the weird thing is there are hardly any food shops.

At the orphanage I used to spend hours in class daydreaming about all the food shops in our street. The cake shop next to the ice-cream shop next to the roast meat shop next to the jelly and jam shop next to the fried potato shop next to the chocolate-covered licorice bullet shop.

Was I making all that up?

Something else is different too.

Dawn was ages ago but there's nobody out and

about. Our street used to be crowded as soon as it got light. People doing things and going places even though they were still yawning. Farm animals complaining because they didn't like being on the cobbles. Kids pinching things from market stalls.

This is very different.

The whole street is deserted.

I walk along from the corner wondering if my memory is wrong. That can happen when you're hungry and tired and your feet hurt because your shoes are too big.

Perhaps I'm confused. Perhaps I'm remembering all the stories I've made up about our noisy crowded street. Perhaps I made the crowds up too.

Then I see it.

Our shop, there on the next corner, and I know I haven't made that up.

Everything's the same. The peeling green paint on the door, the metal post for customers to lean their bikes on, the front step where Szymon Glick threw up as he was leaving my fifth birthday party.

And there's not a single Nazi burn mark anywhere on the shop.

I feel very relieved, but a bit weak from hunger as well and I have to stop and hold onto the wall of Mr Rosenfeld's house.

Now I'm so close to home, I'm starting to feel sad.

I wish Mum and Dad were here instead of away somewhere persuading their favourite author to write faster, or trying to sell books on gun safety to soldiers.

I take a deep breath.

I haven't got time to be sad. I've got a plan to carry out. Hide the books before the Nazis get here. Then I'll have plenty of time to find a railway receipt and be reunited with Mum and Dad.

First I've got to get into the shop.

I walk over and try the door. It's locked. I'm not surprised. Mum's dad was a locksmith before he was killed in a ferry-sinking accident. Mum's very big on locks, except on toilet doors in ferries.

I peer in through the shop window. If I have to smash my way in, I must make sure the flying bits don't damage the books.

I stare for a long time. I have to because when you're shocked and horrified and feeling sick, your eyes don't work very well, even with glasses.

There aren't any books.

All the books in the shop are gone.

The shelves are still there, but no books.

Just old coats. And hats. And underwear.

I can't believe it. The Nazis can't have burnt the books already or the lock would be broken and there would be ash and weeping customers everywhere.

Have Mum and Dad changed their business to second-hand clothes? Never. They love books too much. Mum's not interested in clothes, she was always saying that to Mrs Glick.

Have I got the wrong shop?

I kneel at the front door.

It is the right shop. Here are my initials where I scratched them in the green paint the day before I went to the orphanage so the other kids around here wouldn't forget me.

What's going on?

Have Mum and Dad hidden the books?

Suddenly I hear voices coming from our flat over the shop. A man and a woman.

Thank you God and the others.

'Mum,' I yell. 'Dad.'

Mum and Dad stop talking. But they don't reply. They don't even open the window. I can see their faint shapes, moving behind the curtains.

Why aren't they flinging the windows open and yelling with joy?

Of course. It's been three years and eight months. My voice has changed. I look different. Plus I'm wearing a rabbit hunter's clothes. They'll recognise me once they see my notebook.

The shop door is locked, so I race round the back and up the steps.

The back door of the flat is open.

'Mum,' I yell, bursting in. 'Dad.'

Then I stop in my tracks.

While I was running up the steps part of me feared our kitchen furniture would be gone, just like the books. But it's all here, exactly where it was. The stove where Mum used to make me carrot soup. The table where I had all my meals and my

41

breadcrumb fights with Dad. The fireplace where Mum and Dad used to give me my bath and dry my book if I dropped it in the water.

'Who are you?' snarls a voice.

I spin round.

Standing in the doorway from the living room, glaring at me, is a woman.

It's not Mum.

Mum is slim with dark hair and a gentle pale face. This woman is muscly with hair like straw. Her face is angry and red. Her neck and arms are too.

I don't know what to say.

'Get out,' shouts the woman.

'Grab him,' says a man who isn't Dad, coming in from the bedroom. 'We'll hand him over.'

I back towards the door.

The man comes at me.

I turn and run down the steps. Halfway down I crash into a kid coming up. As I scramble over him I see his face. He's older than he was, but I still recognise him. Wiktor Radzyn, one of the Polish kids from my class when I went to school here.

I don't stop.

I keep running.

'Clear off, Jew,' yells Wiktor behind me. 'This is our house now.'

They've stopped chasing me.

I crouch in my secret hiding place at the edge of town and listen.

No more yelling.

The crowd that was after me must have given up. They mustn't know about this hollow sentry space in the ancient ruined castle wall. When Dad showed me this place years ago he told me it was our secret, so I never told anybody and he mustn't have either.

Thanks, Dad. And thank you God and the others that I wasn't able to fill it up with books like I'd planned, or there wouldn't be room for me in here.

Through the arrow slit I can see the town people walking back towards their homes. Now they're gone, I'm shaking all over.

Why do they hate me and Mum and Dad so much? They couldn't all have bought books they didn't like.

And why is the Radzyn family living in our place?

Have Mum and Dad sold it to them? Why would they do that? The Radzyns aren't booksellers. Mr Radzyn used to empty toilets. Mrs Radzyn had a stall at the market selling old clothes and underwear. Wiktor Radzyn hates books. When he was in my class, he used to pick his nose and wipe it on the pages.

I lean against the crumbling stone wall of my little cave and have a very sad thought. Wiktor has my room now. My bed and my desk and my chair and my oil lamp and my bookshelf and my books.

I think of him lying on the bed, blowing his nose on one of my books.

Then I have a much happier thought.

America.

Of course.

The visas for America must have come through. The ones Mum and Dad tried to get before I went to the orphanage. That's why they've sold the shop, so they can open another one in America. Dad told me a story about a Jewish bookseller in America once. The bookshelves there are solid gold.

Oh no.

Mum and Dad must be on their way to the orphanage to pick me up. Doesn't matter. They won't leave without me. I can be back at the orphanage in two days, two and a bit to allow for walking up the mountain.

Of course, that's probably where all the books are. Mum and Dad have taken them up to Mother Minka so she can buy the ones she wants before they ship the rest off to America.

Phew, I'm feeling much calmer now.

It all makes sense.

I wipe the sweat off my glasses, repack my rags and my feet into my shoes, and wriggle out through the thick undergrowth covering the entrance to the sentry space.

Then I freeze.

Somebody's behind me. I just heard the grass rustle.

I turn around.

Two little kids are staring me, a boy and a girl, barefoot in the dust.

'We're playing grabbing Jews in the street,' says the little boy.

'I'm a Jew,' says the little girl. 'He's a Nazi. He's going to grab me and take me away. Who do you want to be?'

I don't say anything.

'You be a Nazi,' says the little girl, squinting at me in the sunlight.

I shake my head.

'Alright, you be a Jew,' she says. 'That means you have to be sad 'cause the Nazis took your mum and dad away.'

I stare at her.

She gives an impatient sigh.

'All the Jew people got taken,' she says. 'My dad told me. So you have to be sad, alright?'

Relax, I tell myself. It's just a game.

But panic is churning inside me.

'He doesn't want to play,' says the little boy.

The little boy's right, I don't.

I stand outside Mr Rosenfeld's house, doing what I've been doing for hours. Hoping desperately that the little girl is wrong.

Little kids are wrong quite a bit in my experience. There was a little kid at the orphanage who thought you could eat ants.

That's why I've waited until dark and crept back into town. Mr Rosenfeld is Jewish. If he's still here, that'll prove all the Jewish people haven't been taken away.

I knock on Mr Rosenfeld's door.

Silence.

I knock again.

Silence.

That doesn't mean he's not here. He could be reading and concentrating very hard. Or asleep with lots of wax in his ears. Or in the bath and naked.

I knock again, louder.

'Mr Rosenfeld,' I call softly. 'It's Felix Salinger. I need to ask you something. It's urgent. Don't be shy if you're in the bath, I've seen Dad undressed.'

Silence.

Hands grab me from behind. I try to yell, but one of the hands is over my mouth. I'm dragged backwards over the cobbles, into the alley next to Mr Rosenfeld's house.

'Are you crazy?' hisses a man's voice in my ear.

It's not Mr Rosenfeld.

I squirm round and look up.

I can't see the man's face in the dark.

'They're all gone,' he says. 'Rosenfeld, your parents, all of them.'

I want him to stop. I want him to tell me it's just a story.

I try to bite his hand.

'They've all been transported to the city,' he says.

I try again. This time my teeth sink in a bit. The man pulls his hand away. And clamps it back on, harder.

'That's why those weasel Radzyns are living in your house,' says the man. 'That's why Rosenfeld's favourite brown hat is for sale in their shop. And most of the other things he left behind.'

Fear stabs through me. He's right. I did see Mr Rosenfeld's hat in the shop.

I squirm round again.

The moon has come out.

I can see the man's face. It's Mr Kopek. He used to empty toilets with Mr Radzyn.

'You shouldn't be here,' says Mr Kopek. 'Bad time for you lot around here. If I was one of you I'd go and hide in the mountains.'

Suddenly he lets go of me.

'If they get you,' he says, 'we never spoke.'

I understand what he's saying.

'Don't worry,' I reply. 'The Nazis won't be interested in me. I haven't got any books. I lent all mine to a friend.'

Mr Kopek stares at me for a moment, then stuffs something under my arm and hurries away down the alley.

I'm too shaky to stay standing up, so I sit down on the cobbles. I take the package from under my arm. It's wrapped in greaseproof paper. Inside is a piece of bread and a bottle of water.

I don't understand. Why are some people kind

to us Jewish book owners and some people hate us? I wish I'd asked Mr Kopek to explain. And also to tell me why the Nazis hate Jewish books so much that they've dragged Mum and Dad and all their Jewish customers off to the city.

I tell myself a story about a bunch of kids in another country whose parents work in a book warehouse and one day a big pile of Jewish books topples onto the kids' parents and crushes them and the kids vow that when they grow up they'll get revenge on all Jewish books and their owners.

It doesn't feel like a very believable story.

It'll have to do for now, though. Perhaps while I'm on my way to find Mum and Dad I'll be able to think up a better one.

I carefully wrap the bread and the bottle of water again.

I'll need them.

It's a long journey to the city.

Once I walked as fast as I could towards the city to find Mum and Dad and I didn't let anything stop me.

Not until the fire.

I slow down, staring at the horizon.

The fire is miles away, but I can see the flames clearly as they flicker in the darkness. They must be huge. If that's a pile of burning books, there must be millions.

I stop.

I wipe my glasses and try to see if any Nazis are over there. I can't. It's too far away to see people, let alone armbands.

I can hear trucks or cars, though, and faint shouting voices.

Part of me wants to run away, just in case. Another part of me wants to go closer. Mum and Dad might be there. This might be where all the Jewish book owners have been taken, so the Nazis can burn all their books in one big pile.

I go closer.

I don't want to stay on the road in case I bump into any Nazis who are running late, so I cut across some fields.

One of the fields has cabbages in it. As I get closer to the fire, the cabbages are starting to get warm. Some are starting to smell like they're cooking. But I don't stop and eat any.

I can see what's burning now.

It's not books, it's a house.

I still can't see any people, so I stuff the bread and water inside my shirt and take my hat off and pee on it and put it back on to keep my head from blistering and go even closer in case there are some people inside who need to be rescued. I wrote a story once about Mum and Dad rescuing an ink salesman from a burning house, so I know a bit about it.

Blinking from the heat and the glare, I reach the wire fence that separates the house from the fields. The wire is too hot to touch. I wriggle under it.

The lawn is covered with dead chickens. Poor things, they must be cooked. That's what I think until I see the holes in them.

They've been shot.

The owners must have done it to put them out of their misery.

Then I see the owners.

Oh.

They're lying on the lawn next to the chickens, a man and a woman. The man is in pyjamas and the woman is wearing a nightdress. They're both in the same twisted positions as the chickens and both lying in patches of blood.

I want to run away but I don't. Instead, I pick up a chicken feather and hold it in front of the woman's mouth and nose. It's how you tell if people are dead. I read it in a book once.

The feather doesn't move.

It doesn't move with the man either.

I'm shivering in the heat. I've never seen real dead people before. Real dead people are different to dead people in stories. When you see real dead people you want to cry.

I sit on the lawn, the flames from the house drying my tears before they're halfway down my face.

These poor people must be Jewish book owners who couldn't bear to let the Nazis burn their books so they put up a struggle and to pay them back the Nazis killed them and their chickens and set fire to their whole house.

Please Mum and Dad, I beg silently.

Don't be like these people.

Don't put up a struggle.

It's only books.

Behind me part of the house collapses, bombarding me and the poor dead book owners with sparks and burning ash. My skin stings. My clothes start to smoulder. I roll across the lawn to put them out. And stop with my face close to another person.

It's a girl, about six years old, lying on her side.

A little kid. What sort of people would kill a little kid just for the sake of some books?

A horrible thought grows in my throbbing head. What if us Jews aren't being bullied just because of books? What if it's because of something else?

Then I notice that the little girl isn't bleeding.

Gently I roll her over.

The fire behind me is burning bright as day and I can see that the girl's pyjamas don't have any holes in them at all. Not from ash or bullets. The only medical condition I can find is a big bruise on her forehead.

I grab a feather and hold it in front of her face, but I don't need to because when I crouch closer I can hear the snot rattling in her nose.

It's loud, but not as loud as the car engine noise I suddenly hear in the distance.

I peer over towards the road.

Coming along it fast are two black cars. They look just like the Nazi cars that came to the orphanage.

The Nazis must be coming back here to the scene of their crime to get rid of the evidence. I've read about this type of criminal behaviour in stories.

I haul the unconscious girl up onto my back and stagger through the smoke and sparks towards the fence. The hot wire burns my arm as I squeeze through, but I don't care. I just want to get me and this poor orphan safely hidden in the cabbages.

'What's your name?' I ask the girl for about the hundredth time as we trudge along the dark road.

Actually it's just me doing the trudging. She's still on my back, her arms round my neck.

As usual she doesn't reply. The only way I know she's awake and not unconscious is when I look over my shoulder at her and see the moonlight gleaming in her dark eyes.

This is killing me. The longest I've ever carried anyone before was Dodie in the piggyback race on sports day. That was only once around the playing field.

I try to take my mind off the pain in my arms by thinking about good things.

Mum's smell.

The way Dad's hair falls into his eyes when he's reading.

How at least this kid isn't getting overexcited like Dodie and kicking me in the ribs.

The pain in my arms is still bad. I wonder how much longer I can keeping going without dropping her.

Then I see something.

Is that a haystack?

It's a bit hard to tell because the moon's gone behind a cloud, but I'm pretty sure that big dark shape behind that hedge is a haystack.

Suddenly I can't resist it.

I know it's risky. The Nazis could be coming along here any time. But I can't go on. My legs are hurting too now.

'I need a rest,' I say to the girl.

She doesn't reply.

I push through the hedge and drag armfuls of hay off the haystack with one arm and make a bed on the ground. I lay the girl down on it as gently as I can and put some hay over her to keep her warm. Then I lay down next to her. I don't bother with top hay for me, I'm too tired.

The girl stands up and starts crying.

'Where's my mummy and daddy?' she wails.

It's the first thing she's said since she stopped being unconscious and it's the thing I've been dreading most.

'I want my mummy and daddy,' she howls.

At least I've had plenty of time to make a plan.

'I want mine too,' I say. 'That's why we're going to the city.'

Keep her hopeful, that's the plan. She's had a nasty bang on the head. I can't tell her the terrible news while she's not well. Later on, when she's feeling better and I've found Mum and Dad, that'll be the time to let her know her parents are dead. Because then Mum can do it. And then we can take her to live with Mother Minka.

'Who are you?' sobs the girl.

'I'm Felix.' I say. 'Who are you?'

'I want Mummy,' she wails.

'Don't yell,' I beg her. 'We have to be quiet.'

She carries on wailing. I can't tell her that the reason we have to be quiet is because the Nazis might hear us. That would terrify her. So I make something up.

'Shhhh,' I say. 'We'll wake the sheep.'

Then I remember there aren't any sheep. The fields are all empty.

Still sobbing, the girl looks at me like I used to look at Marek when he tried to tell me his parents were professional fighters who died in a wrestling accident.

I get up and go over to her and kneel down so my face is level with hers. I put my hand gently on her arm. I wish my hand was bigger, like Mother Minka's.

'I'm scared too,' I say quietly. 'I want my mum and dad too. That's why we're going to the city.'

I gently touch her forehead, next to the bruise.

'Does it hurt?' I ask.

She nods, more tears rolling out of her eyes.

'My mum's very good with hurt heads,' I say. 'When you meet her tomorrow she'll make it stop hurting.'

'Your hat smells,' says the girl, but she's not sobbing so much.

I flop back down on the hay.

'If you lie down and have a rest,' I say, 'I'll tell you a story about your mummy and daddy taking you on a picnic.'

The girl looks at me. She sticks her bottom lip out.

'We don't go on picnics,' she says. 'Don't you know anything?'

'Alright,' I say. 'You and your mummy and daddy flying in an aeroplane.'

'We don't fly in aeroplanes,' she says.

I sigh. I feel really sorry for her. It's really hard being an orphan if you haven't got an imagination.

I try one more time.

'Alright,' I say. 'I'll tell you a story about a kid who spends three years and eight months living in a castle in the mountains.'

She gives me that look again.

I give up. I roll over and close my eyes. I've done my best. I'm so tired I don't care any more.

Then I feel her lying down next to me.

I sigh again. A promise is a promise. I roll over and face her.

'Once,' I say, 'there was a boy called William –'

'No,' she interrupts, pointing to herself. 'I'm a girl. My name's Zelda. Don't you know anything?'

Once I woke up and I was at home in bed. Dad was reading me a story about a boy who got left in an orphanage. Mum came in with some carrot soup. They both promised they'd never leave me anywhere. We hugged and hugged.

Then I really wake up and I'm in a haystack.

Hay stalks are stabbing me through my clothes. Cold damp air is making my face feel clammy. The early morning sun is hurting my eyes. A young girl is shaking me and complaining.

'I'm hungry,' she's saying.

I feel around for my glasses, put them on, look at her groggily, and remember.

Zelda, the girl with the dead parents.

And the bossy attitude. She made me tell her the castle in the mountains story about ten times last night, till I got it right.

'I need to do a pee,' she says.

'Alright,' I mumble. 'First a pee, then breakfast.'

We both do a pee behind the haystack. Then I unwrap the bread and water. Zelda has a drink and I have a sip. I break her off a piece of bread and a smaller one for me. She needs extra because she's injured. The bruise on her forehead is dark now, and there's a lump.

'Your hat still smells,' says Zelda.

I open my mouth to explain why firefighters often have smelly hats, then close it again. Best not to remind her that her house has burnt down.

'Sorry,' I say.

Zelda is frowning and screwing up her face, and I don't think it's just because of my hat.

'Are you alright?' I ask.

'My head hurts,' she says. 'Don't you know anything?'

'It'll feel better when we get to the city,' I say. I don't mention Mum's healing powers this time in case it makes her wail for her parents again.

My head hurts too.

It's hot and throbbing. Last night when it started hurting I thought it was just overheated from the fire. But it can't be that now because my skin is cold and clammy.

I'm hearing things too, which can happen when you've got a fever. I can hear voices and footsteps and the rumble of cartwheels. I must still be half-asleep, dreaming about our street on market day.

No I'm not.

I'm wide awake. The sounds are real. They're

coming from the road on the other side of the hedge.

'Stay here,' I whisper to Zelda.

'What is it?' she says, alarmed.

'I'll be back in a minute,' I say. 'Then we'll go to the city.'

'To see our mums and dads,' says Zelda.

I run to the hedge, wriggle into the leaves and branches, and peer out at the road. And gawk in amazement. The road is crowded with people. Men and women and kids and old people. A hundred or even more. They're all walking wearily in the direction of the city. Most of them are carrying bundles or bags or suitcases or cooking pots. A few are carrying books.

Each person is wearing an armband over their coat or jacket. Not a red and black armband like the Nazis had at the orphanage, these are white with a blue star, a Jewish star like on some of the Jewish houses at home. Must be so these travellers can recognise the other members of their group. We used to have paper saints pinned to our tops on sports day so everyone could see which dormitory we were from.

A sudden loud noise makes me shrink back into the hedge.

Several soldiers on bikes with motors are driving up and down, yelling and waving at the people in a foreign language. The soldiers have all got guns. None of the people have. The soldiers seem to want the people to go faster.

With a jolt I understand.

These soldiers are Nazis. This straggling crowd of people are all Jewish book owners, all being transported to the city.

Are Mum and Dad here?

I lean forward again, trying to see, but before I can spot them I hear a sound behind me.

A scream.

Zelda.

I struggle out of the hedge, almost losing my glasses. I jam them back on and almost faint at what I see.

Zelda is standing by the haystack, rigid with fear. Next to her, pointing a machine gun down at her head, is a Nazi soldier.

'Don't shoot,' I scream, running over to them.

The soldier points his gun at me.

I freeze. With a stab of panic I see my notebook lying in the hay at his feet. It must have fallen out of my shirt. The Nazi soldier must have seen it. He must think we're Jewish book owners. Disobedient ones, like Zelda's parents.

My throat goes dry with fear.

'That isn't really a book,' I croak. 'It's a notebook. And it isn't hers, it's mine. And I wasn't trying to hide it. I was planning to hand it over as soon as we get to the city and find the place where the books are being burnt.'

The soldier stares at me like he doesn't believe what I've just said.

Desperately I try to think of a way to make friends with him.

'Sorry I just shouted at you,' I say. 'I'm from the mountains where you have to shout and yodel to make yourself heard. Can you yodel?'

The soldier doesn't reply. He just scowls and waves his gun towards the hedge.

I grab Zelda by the hand, and my notebook, and the bread and water.

Zelda is trembling just as much as me.

'Come on,' I say to her gently. 'He's telling us we have to go to the city with all the other people.'

'To see our mums and dads,' says Zelda to the soldier.

You know how when you're looking for your mum and dad in a straggling crowd of people trudging along a dusty road and you speed up and get to the front and then slow down and drop to the back and you still can't see them even when you pray to God, Jesus, the Virgin Mary, the Pope and Adolf Hitler?

That's happening to me.

My head is throbbing and I feel squashed with disappointment.

I try to cheer myself up by thinking how Mum and Dad have probably already arrived at the city and are having a sit down and taking the weight off their feet.

It doesn't cheer me up much. The Nazi soldiers on the motorbikes are still yelling at everyone. I hope Mum and Dad haven't got noisy cross soldiers like these. Mum gets very indignant when people are rude, and sometimes she tells them off.

Zelda doesn't look very happy either.

'My feet hurt,' she says.

Poor thing. She's only wearing fluffy bedtime slippers. The soles aren't thick enough to protect her feet from the stones on the road.

I bend down and pull some of the rag stuffing out of my shoes.

'Come on,' I say to Zelda. 'Piggyback.'

She jumps on my back.

'Hold on tight,' I say, and start walking again so the soldiers won't yell at us for lagging behind.

Some of the other kids walking with their mums and dads give Zelda jealous looks. I don't blame them. Some of them are only about three or four. Their mums and dads are too weary to talk to them, let alone carry them.

I can see Zelda wants to stay on my back till we get to the city. I wish she could, but I feel too ill.

I take her slippers off, wind the rags round her feet and put her slippers back on.

'There,' I say. 'That should help.'

I put her back down.

'It feels funny,' she says after a few steps.

I try to think of something to help her get used to it.

'All the great travellers in history had rags round their feet,' I say. 'Christopher Columbus who discovered America, he had rags round his feet. Doctor Livingstone in Africa, he did. Hannibal the Great, he did too. So did his elephants. In the future, by the year 1960, I think they'll make shoes with rags already in them.'

Zelda gives me one of her looks.

'By the year 1960,' she says, 'people won't need shoes. They'll have wheels instead of feet. Don't you know anything?'

'Sorry,' I say. 'I forgot.'

'Why do those people look so sad,' asks Zelda.

I've been expecting her to ask. She's been staring in a concerned way at the people walking with us. An elderly woman near us is crying and Zelda's been looking at her a lot.

I'm not sure what to say.

Zelda squeezes my hand even tighter than usual.

'Well?' she demands. 'Why do they?'

I know why the people look sad. They've been walking for hours and they're tired and hungry and worried about their books and parents, just like us. We probably look sad to them.

But I don't say this to Zelda. When a little kid doesn't even know her parents are dead, you've got to try and keep her spirits up.

'They're feeling sad because they haven't got rags in their shoes,' I say to her. 'They'll be much happier when we get to the city.'

I'm about to tell Zelda about the rag shops that are probably in the city when I see something out of the corner of my eye.

The elderly woman has just fainted at the side of the road. She's lying in the dust. Nobody is stopping to help her. Not the other Jewish people, not the soldiers, not me.

I can't give anyone else a piggyback. I can't even lift Zelda, the way I feel now.

'What's wrong with that lady?' asks Zelda.

I tell her that the lady is just having a rest, and after we've gone a farmer will come and take the lady home and she'll live happily on the farm with his family and become very good at milking cows and in the year 1972 she'll invent a machine that milks them automatically and also makes butter.

Zelda thinks about this.

'In 1972,' says Zelda, 'cows will make their own butter. Don't you know anything?'

I'm tempted to say, 'No, I don't. Not any more.'

I look around at the tired hungry sick Jewish people staggering along the road. An awful question has been throbbing in my head for ages now. It's the question I first thought of when I saw Zelda lying on her lawn.

Why would the Nazis make people suffer like this just for the sake of some books?

I need to try and find an answer.

'Excuse me,' I say to a man walking nearby. 'Are you a book lover?'

The man stares at me as if I'm mad. His grey sagging face was miserable before, but now he looks like he's close to tears. He looks away. I feel terrible. I wish I hadn't asked.

Not just because I've made a suffering Jewish man feel upset at the sight of a crazy kid. Also because I've got a horrible suspicion I know the answer to the question.

Maybe it's not just our books the Nazis hate.

Maybe it's us.

Once I spent about six hours telling stories to Zelda, to keep her spirits up, to keep my spirits up, to keep our legs moving as we trudge through the rain towards the city.

At least the rain is washing my hat, but my head is still hot and throbbing. Every time a Nazi soldier yells at me or at another person in our soggy straggling group, my head has stabs of pain.

Me and Zelda have eaten our bread and we're both hungry. As we trudge on I keep my eyes open for food. Nothing, just dark wet trees and big fields full of mud and wet grass.

I keep thinking about Mum and Dad and hoping they're not this hungry, but worrying about them only makes my head throb more.

'Why have you stopped the story?' says Zelda.

'Sorry,' I say. I'm telling her a story about how much fun kids can have in the city, but my imagination is as tired and hungry as my body, and my shirt's wet and I'm worried my notebook is getting ruined.

Zelda is looking annoyed. I don't blame her. Her pyjamas are as sodden as my shirt.

'Keep going with the story,' she says. 'William and Violet Elizabeth are in the big cake shop at the zoo. Remember?'

'I remember,' I say. 'Did I tell you about the elephants? The ones that float in by parachute with the extra supplies of cakes?'

'Yes,' says Zelda crossly. 'Don't you know anything?'

I'm being distracted again. Another straggling crowd of Jewish people have appeared out of a side road and are walking with us now. They look terrible. Some of them have got bigger bruises than Zelda.

Zelda's so exhausted she hasn't even asked me about them, but I can see she's noticed and she's as concerned as I am.

Somehow I find the energy to carry on with the story.

'William and Violet Elizabeth eat another six cakes each,' I continue. 'Then suddenly a zoo keeper rushes in, upset and yelling. A vicious gorilla has escaped and is on a violent rampage across Poland.'

'Across the whole world,' says Zelda.

'Yes,' I say, glad I've got her mind off the bruised people. 'So William and Violet Elizabeth come up with a plan to capture the gorilla.'

'Violet Elizabeth comes up with most of it,' says Zelda.

'Alright,' I say. 'The plan is, they go to a luxury hotel and get a luxury hotel room and put lots of things in it that gorillas like. Bananas. Coconuts. Small roasted monkeys.'

I can see Zelda isn't happy with this.

'Why do they put the things in a hotel room?' she asks.

'Because,' I say, 'luxury hotels in cities are made of a modern invention called concrete which is super strong. Even a gorilla can't bash his way out when he's locked in a concrete room.'

'The gorilla might be a girl,' says Zelda.

I look at her wearily.

'He might,' I say. 'Anyway, William and Violet Elizabeth send a message to the gorilla about the hotel room, then hide in the wardrobe with a big net.'

'And toys,' says Zelda.

I look at her, puzzled.

'Gorillas like toys,' she says.

I know I should be agreeing with her, but I don't, partly because I'm not sure if gorillas do like toys, and partly because what I'm seeing ahead of us is suddenly making it hard for me to speak.

One of the people in our group, the man who isn't a book lover, has started yelling at the soldiers, screaming hysterically. Suddenly a soldier hits the man in the face with a machine gun. The man falls down. The soldiers start kicking him. People cry out. I almost do myself.

Instead I step between the man and Zelda so she won't see. I put my arm round her shoulder and walk as fast as I can, talking loudly to distract her.

'William and Violet Elizabeth's plan is a big success,' I say, 'because when the gorilla hears about the toys, he rampages straight to the hotel.'

'I think it's a silly plan,' says Zelda.

I'm struggling to stay calm. Behind us I can still hear the poor man grunting as the soldiers kick him.

'Tell me a better plan,' I say.

'Well,' says Zelda. 'Violet Elizabeth and William dig a big hole, like those people over there, and the gorilla falls into it.'

I look over to where Zelda is pointing. In a patch of forest near the road a big crowd of people, hundreds it looks like, are digging what looks like a huge hole.

I stare, confused.

It's hard to see because of the trees, but the people don't look like farm workers. Some of them look like children. Some of them look very old. Some of them look like they might be naked. And I think I can see soldiers pointing guns at them.

'What are they doing?' says Zelda.

I wait for my imagination to come up with something.

It doesn't.

'Maybe a gorilla has really escaped,' says Zelda.

She puts her arm round my waist. I keep mine round her shoulders.

Some of the people in our group are stopping, trying to see what's going on in the forest. The soldiers are yelling at us to keep moving.

We trudge on through the rain.

'The gorilla has a friend,' says Zelda. 'A kind man. He doesn't want the gorilla to be captured, so he tells the army to leave the gorilla alone and they hit him with a gun.'

I look down at Zelda. I can tell from the sadness on her face that she did see the man being hit.

I squeeze her tighter.

'That's a good story,' I say. 'And when the man gets better, he and the gorilla go and live happily in the jungle and open a cake shop.'

'Yes,' says Zelda quietly.

She doesn't look as though she totally believes it.

I don't either.

The city isn't anything like it is in stories.

The wide streets are dirty and the tall buildings, five levels high some of them, have all got Nazi flags hanging off the balconies and out of the windows.

Army trucks and tanks are parked everywhere and lots of soldiers are standing around telling each other foreign jokes and laughing.

There's no sign of a zoo and I haven't seen a single cake shop or rag shop and the local people are really unfriendly. Lots of them are standing on the footpaths yelling unkind things at us as we straggle past.

Dirty Jews.

Stuff like that.

Of course we're dirty. We've been walking for nearly a whole day in the rain.

I'm looking around for Mum and Dad, but I can't see them. Zelda is doing the same. I hope I find mine before she realises hers aren't here.

Where are you, Mum and Dad?

I must try and be patient. That's what Mum used to tell me when I was little and I got upset because I couldn't read any of the words in Dad's big book about two thousand years of Jewish history.

This is hopeless. There are too many people. I've never seen so many people in one place. And all the Jewish people look as unhappy as us, huddled and weary in dark damp coats and blankets trying to ignore the rude things the city people are shouting at us.

'I don't like the city,' says Zelda.

I wish I knew what to say.

I wish I could tell her a story to make us all feel better. But I'm too exhausted and my feet are too blistered.

We're heading for a big brick wall built right across the street. That's a very strange place to build a wall. There's a gate in the wall with soldiers guarding it and the people ahead of us are going through the gate.

No they're not, not all of them.

The soldiers are grabbing some of the Jewish people. They're giving them buckets and scrubbing brushes. They're making them kneel down and scrub the cobblestones.

This is terrible.

The city council should pay people to clean the streets, not make visitors do it while the locals stand around laughing.

I hope Mum and Dad didn't have to do this.

Oh no, what now?

This is even more terrible.

Soldiers are grabbing Jewish kids and throwing them into the back of a truck. It looks like no kids are allowed through the gate. People are screaming and crying as their kids are snatched away.

What's going on?

Why are the Nazis separating the kids from the adults?

I don't want to be separated, I want to stay here and find Mum and Dad.

I pull Zelda over to the side of the street. I look around for an alley we can run down. The local people are pointing at us and yelling at the soldiers that we're Jews and we're escaping.

What was that noise?

Gunshots.

Everyone is screaming.

Over by the wall two people are lying on the ground bleeding. Another man is wrestling with a soldier, trying to get to a kid that another soldier is holding. The soldier with the kid points a pistol and shoots the man.

Oh.

The screaming is even louder now, but I can still hear Zelda howling in fright.

I try to cling onto her. Too late. Somebody is dragging her away from me.

A Nazi officer with a bored look on his face is holding her by the hair and pointing a gun at her.

'Please don't,' I croak.

I wait for my imagination to come up with a reason I can tell him why he mustn't shoot her, but my head is burning and everything is spinning round and I fall down shouting but not words.

The cobblestones hurt my face. Gunshots hurt my ears. I start crying. I don't know what to do.

I haven't got any more stories.

Once I lay in the street in tears because the Nazis are everywhere and no grown-ups can protect kids from them, not Mum and Dad, not Mother Minka, not Father Ludwik, not God, not Jesus, not the Virgin Mary, not the Pope, not Adolf Hitler.

Then I look up and see that I'm wrong.

Here's one doing it now.

A big man in a scuffed leather jacket has his hand on Zelda's shoulder and is pleading with the Nazi officer in a foreign language. I think he's speaking Nazi. Which is strange because he's wearing a Jewish armband.

The Nazi officer lets go of Zelda's hair and raises his gun and points it at the man's head.

The man doesn't weep or grovel. He lifts up the leather bag he's carrying, which is also fairly scuffed, and holds it in front of the Nazi officer's face.

Why is he doing that?

The Nazi officer glances at the bag, still looking

bored. He raises his other hand, grabs a tuft of the man's beard and twists it hard with his leather glove. The man stands there and lets him.

The local people watching all laugh and cheer.

The man looks sad, but ignores them.

After a very long twist, the Nazi officer turns and walks away. He goes over to the crowd of Jewish people who are still crying and shouting because some of them have been shot and their children are still being put into the truck.

He goes up behind a woman and points his gun at the back of her head.

I try to scramble up so I can go over and stop the Nazi officer.

I can't stay on my feet. I'm too dizzy. I fall back down onto my knees.

The Nazi officer shoots the woman.

Oh.

Zelda screams.

The man turns her away from the horrible sight and starts to take her off through the crowd of gawking locals.

'No,' yells Zelda. 'I'm not going without Felix.'

She struggles and kicks. The man turns and stares at me. He looks very weary, as if having his beard twisted and seeing innocent people being shot to death is bad enough and the last thing he needs is a kid who can't stand up and has just started vomiting.

I try to tell him I'm looking for my mum and

dad, but more vomit comes out and the whole street goes spinning away from me.

I wake up with a painful light flickering in my eyes.

It's a candle flame.

Mother Minka always has a candle when she comes into the dormitory at night to give Marek a detention for going to bed with no pyjamas on or to whack Borys for throwing Marek's pyjamas out the window or to –

I sit up in panic.

Am I back in the orphanage?

I don't want to be. I need to find Mum and Dad. I need to warn them. I need to –

A big hairy hand pushes me gently back down. It's not Mother Minka's.

A man with a beard is looking down at me, frowning. I've seen him somewhere before.

'Are you Father Ludwik?' I say.

My throat hurts. My skin is burning.

The man shakes his head. He wipes my face with a damp cloth.

'Try and rest,' he says.

I can see now he isn't Father Ludwik but I don't know who else he could be. Then I remember. The man with the magic bag. But he's not speaking Nazi any more.

Suddenly a girl is looking down at me too.

'He's Barney,' she says. 'Don't you know anything?'

I know who the girl is, but before I can say her name everything spins away again.

I wake up in darkness.

Panic smothers me.

'My notebook,' I yell. 'I've lost my notebook.'

My throat still hurts. My whole body feels cold. Except my head. It's on fire.

Somebody lights a candle.

A silver heart is glinting in front of my eyes. It's on a chain, hanging from the girl Zelda's neck as she looks down at me, concerned.

'He thinks he's lost his notebook,' she says.

The man who's not Father Ludwik is also looking down at me, also concerned.

'Your notebook is safe,' he says.

'So are your letters,' says Zelda. 'We threw your hat away.'

'Here,' says the man. 'Drink.'

He puts a metal cup to my lips. I sip some water. It makes me cough, which makes my head hurt a lot.

'Is Felix going to die?' whispers Zelda to the man.

The man doesn't say anything, just looks more worried.

Now my head feels even worse. I have to find Mum and Dad. They know how to make me better.

I remember the Nazis have got them.

Panic swamps me again.

If only Mum and Dad hadn't put me in that stupid orphanage. If only they'd let me stay with them. I could have protected them. Somehow.

I want to sit up, to ask the man to help me find them, but I'm so weak and giddy I don't know where up is.

Far off I can hear Zelda demanding to know if I'm going to die.

'Please,' I whisper to the darkness. 'Find my parents.'

I hope the man can hear me.

'They're in danger,' I croak. 'Really bad danger. Don't believe the notebook. The stories in the notebook aren't true.'

I wake up to the sound of someone crying.

It's not me.

'I want to go home,' sobs a kid's voice.

Zelda?

No, it's a boy.

I open my eyes. A few thin needles of daylight are stabbing through the dark. They make my eyes sting but I don't feel like I'm burning up any more and my head doesn't hurt so much.

I put my glasses on but I can't see much in the gloom. My bed is a sack stuffed with something soft. Next to me is another sack bed with a crying boy on it. He looks about five.

The man who's not Father Ludwik crouches down and gives the boy a hug.

'I want to go home, Barney,' sobs the boy.

'I know,' says the man.

'I miss them,' says the boy.

The man gently smooths the boy's hair.

'I know, Henryk,' he says. 'One day you'll be with your mummy and daddy. Until then I'll look after you, I promise.'

The boy sniffs, but he's stopped crying.

'Cry some more if you want to,' says the man. 'Ruth will hold you.'

A girl about my age with curly hair steps forward and puts an arm round the boy.

The boy wipes his face on his sleeve.

'I've finished now,' he says.

Barney turns to me and puts his hand on my forehead.

'Good,' he says. 'Much better. You're doing well, Felix.'

He hands me a metal cup with something hot in it.

Soup.

I put the cup down, roll over angrily and close my eyes.

This man Barney is an idiot.

You don't tell a kid he'll find his parents one day. One day doesn't mean anything. If you don't know when they're coming, you let the kid go and look for them now.

I want to shout at the man, but I don't because Dodie reckons it's pointless shouting at idiots, plus

79

it would probably hurt my throat.

Instead I ignore the man's hand on my back and try to tell myself a story to cheer myself up. A story about a kid who finds his parents in a city and takes them to a desert island with cake shops where they live happily ever after.

It's no good.

When I close my eyes all I can see is Nazi soldiers shooting people, including kids who just want a lift on a country road.

What if Mum and Dad waved to an army truck on their way the city?

I don't want to think about it.

If you tell yourself stories like that you could end up crying.

'Felix.'

A hand is shaking me gently. I keep my eyes closed for a while, then open them.

Barney is crouching by my bed. He's holding my notebook.

'Felix,' he says. 'Do you mind if I read one of your stories to the others?'

I put my glasses on and look around, squinting in the candlelight.

My bed is surrounded.

There's Barney and Zelda and the little boy who was crying and the girl with the curly hair. There's also a boy a bit younger than me who's chewing the end of a piece of wood, a girl a bit older than me with a bandaged arm, a toddler with half its hair missing, and a boy about my age who's blinking his eyes non-stop and hugging the dirtiest teddy bear I've ever seen.

'Just say if you don't want me to,' says Barney. 'We understand if your stories are private. But Zelda has told us what a good storyteller you are, and a few people here have got missing parents, and I think they'd enjoy hearing one.'

'I would,' says the girl with the bandaged arm.

'I would,' says the little boy who was crying.

'I would,' says the girl with curly hair.

'No,' I say.

They all look at me, disappointed.

'Felix,' says Zelda crossly. 'We all want to hear your stories. Don't you know anything?'

Barney puts his hand on my shoulder.

'That's alright, Felix,' he says gently. 'We understand.'

I can feel myself shaking and I know why. The stories in my notebook are stupid. While I was writing them, Mum and Dad were being chased all over Europe by the Nazis. And being captured.

'Those stories are obviously very important to you,' says Barney.

No they're not, I think bitterly. Not any more.

'Anyway,' says Barney. 'We're very glad to have you and Zelda living with us. Aren't we everyone?'

'Yes,' says the girl with the bandaged arm. So does Henryk and the girl with the curly hair and the toddler. The chewing-wood boy just keeps chewing his wood and the blinking boy just keeps blinking.

As I look around at their faces I can see how disappointed they are not to be hearing a story.

Too bad.

'Zelda,' says Barney. 'How about you telling us a story?'

Zelda sits up straight and smooths her tattered dress down over her knees. I'm glad to see she's not still wearing her damp pyjamas.

'Once upon a time,' she says, 'two children lived in a castle in the mountains.'

She pauses, gives me a look to show me she's still cross, then continues.

'Their names were Zelda and William . . .'

Once I was living in a cellar in a Nazi city with seven other kids when I shouldn't have been.

My fever has gone.

I shouldn't be lying in bed, I should be out looking for Mum and Dad.

'Felix,' says Zelda, jumping on my sack. 'Wake up. It's time to wake up. Are you awake?'

'Yes,' I say. 'I am now.'

'You have to get up,' says Zelda. 'You have to tell us a story.'

I don't reply.

'You have to,' insists Zelda. 'Barney said I'm not allowed to any more. He said I start too many arguments. He's wrong, but that's what he said.'

I get up. I'm desperate to pee. While I was sick Barney let me pee in a bottle, but he must have taken it.

'Where's the toilet?' I say.

Zelda points. Through the gloom of the cellar I

can just make out some wooden steps going up in one corner. Behind the steps is a bucket.

I stagger over to it. It's half full and pongs, but I'm desperate.

While I go, Zelda comes over and watches. I want to turn away, but I don't. Orphans deserve a bit of fun.

'Hurry up,' says Zelda. 'We're bored. We want a story.'

When I've finished I look around the cellar, but I can't see the others. There are needles of light pricking through the gloom and I can see several sack beds but no Barney and no other kids.

'Where's Barney?' I say.

'He's out getting us food,' says Zelda.

'Where are the other kids?' I say.

Zelda doesn't reply. I can see she's trying not to giggle. And trying not to look at a big untidy pile of coats in the middle of the cellar floor. The pile of coats seems to be giggling too.

Suddenly the coats fly up into the air. Huddled on the floor in a circle are the other kids, hands over their mouths, laughing themselves silly. Well, most of them are. The wood-chewing boy is just chewing his wood.

I'm not sure what's going on.

'It's a tent,' says Zelda. 'A story tent. Don't you know anything?'

The kids are all laughing at me now.

Suddenly I feel cross. Don't *you* know anything,

I want to yell at them. Our parents are out there in a dangerous Nazi city. The Nazis are shooting people. They could be shooting our parents. A story isn't going to help.

But I don't. It's not their fault. They don't understand what it feels like when you've put your mum and dad in terrible danger. When the only reason they couldn't get a visa to go to America is because when you were six you asked the man at the visa desk if the red blotches on his face were from sticking his head in a dragon's mouth.

'Story,' says little Henryk, clapping his hands.

The others are looking up at me hopefully.

'Sorry,' I say. 'I haven't got time for a story right now. I have to go out.'

'You can't,' says Zelda. 'We're not allowed to.'

I ignore her. I look for the exit. The cellar has stone walls and a stone floor and no windows. The ceiling is made of wooden planks. The long needles of daylight are coming in through gaps between them. Up there must be the way out.

I climb the steps. At the top is a square door in the ceiling planks. The bolt is pulled back. I push the door, but it won't open.

'It's locked on the other side,' says the older girl with the bandaged arm. 'Barney locks it.'

I thump the door in frustration.

'Shhhh,' say most of the kids.

'We have to be quiet,' says Zelda. 'We're hiding.'

'Who from?' I say as I come down the steps.

As soon as I say it, I remember the Nazis putting kids into a truck and I know it's a stupid question.

'Adolf Hitler doesn't like Jewish kids,' says the girl with the curly hair.

'Adolf Hitler?' I say, surprised. 'Father Ludwik says Adolf Hitler is a great man. He's in charge of Poland. He's the prime minister or the king or something.'

Zelda gives me her look.

'Adolf Hitler,' she says, 'is the boss of the Nazis. Don't you know anything?'

I stare at her.

'It's true,' says the blinking boy, blinking harder than ever.

I stare at all the kids, who are all nodding.

If they're right, this is incredible. I wonder if Father Ludwik has heard about this?

'That's why we have to hide,' says the girl with the bandaged arm. 'All the other Jewish kids around here have been taken away by the Nazis. Adolf Hitler's orders. And they never come back. The only kids left are the ones hiding like us.'

'Can we get on with the story now?' says Zelda.

I sit on the floor with them, my thoughts in a daze. Suddenly I'm thinking about another story. The one Mum and Dad told me about why I had to stay at the orphanage. They said it was so I could go to school there while they travelled to fix up their business. They told it so well, that story, I believed it for three years and eight months.

That story saved my life.

Zelda and the others are dragging the coats over our heads and making a tent.

'Tell us another story about the boy in the castle,' says Henryk.

'His name's William,' says Zelda.

'Shhh,' says the girl with the curly hair. She's brushing it with a hairbrush, over and over, which looks pretty painful. She smiles at me. 'Let Felix tell us.'

I try to think of something to tell them. Something to take our minds off our worries. Something to make us forget that the most important man in the whole of Poland hates us and our parents and our books.

'One morning,' I say, 'William wakes up in his castle. In his breakfast soup he finds a magic carrot.'

'A magic carrot,' interrupts Zelda. 'That means he gets three wishes.'

'It doesn't have to be three wishes,' says the blinking boy. 'It could just be one wish.'

'It's three,' says Zelda indignantly. 'If he holds the carrot right.'

I sigh. I'm not in a story mood. My brain is buzzing with too many other things.

'Look,' I say. 'Let's not have another fight. Why doesn't everybody just take it in turns to say what they'd wish for if they had a magic carrot.'

'I'd wish for my mummy and daddy,' says Zelda. 'Three times.'

'Apart from parents,' says the girl with the bandaged arm.

Everyone frowns and thinks hard.

'Tidy hair,' says the girl with curly hair, still brushing it non-stop.

'Your hair is tidy, Ruth,' says the girl with the bandaged arm. 'You've got lovely hair.'

Ruth gives a little smile but carries on brushing.

'What about you, Jacob?' says the girl with the bandaged arm to the blinking boy.

Jacob blinks hard. 'My dog,' he says.

'Me too,' says Henryk. 'And my grandma's dog.'

The girl with the bandaged arm gives the toddler a cuddle. 'What would you like, Janek?'

'Carrot,' says the toddler.

Everyone laughs.

'I'd wish to be alive,' says the girl with the bandaged arm.

Everyone laughs again, except me and the wood-chewing boy.

I don't get it.

'Her name's Chaya,' says Ruth, still brushing. 'It means alive in Hebrew.'

'Your turn,' says Chaya to me.

I can't think of anything except for Mum and Dad. And wishing Zelda's parents were still alive. But I can't say that either. I signal to the wood-chewing boy to have his go.

He doesn't reply. He doesn't even look at me. He

just keeps on chewing the end of the piece of wood in his hands.

'You'd like the rest of your house, eh Moshe?' says Chaya gently.

Moshe nods as he chews, not looking up.

'Come on, Felix,' says Zelda. 'You have to have your turn. Use your imagination.'

I wait for my imagination to come up with something.

Anything.

It doesn't.

All I can think of is that if Adolf Hitler hates Jewish kids, perhaps God and Jesus and the Virgin Mary and the Pope do too.

'He's not going to tell us,' says Ruth.

'Come on,' says Henryk. 'Let's have a lice hunt.'

The kids throw the coats off and go and sit in the needles of daylight and start searching through each other's hair and clothes.

All except Zelda.

'You're mean,' she says to me.

'Sorry,' I say.

I flop down on my bed. My imagination doesn't want to be bothered with stories, not now. All it wants to do is plan how I'm going to get out of this place and find Mum and Dad before Adolf Hitler's Nazis kill them.

Once I escaped from an underground hiding place by telling a story. It was a bit exaggerated. It was a bit fanciful. It was my imagination getting a bit carried away.

It was a lie.

'Barney,' I whisper, tugging his sleeve as he creeps up the cellar steps.

He spins round, startled, and nearly drops his candle. He thought I was asleep like the other kids.

'I need to come with you,' I whisper.

Barney frowns.

I start to explain why I have to go with him.

He puts his finger on his lips and signals for me to follow him up the steps. I climb after him through the doorway in the ceiling. And find myself in a huge room full of dusty old machinery.

Barney puts his leather bag down, gently lowers the trap door and locks it with a padlock.

He sees me looking around and points to the machinery.

'Printing presses,' he says. 'For printing books. Not now. Before.'

I know what he means. Before the Nazis went right off books. And Jews.

'So,' says Barney quietly. 'Why do you need to come with me?'

I take a deep breath.

'I need to find my parents,' I say. 'Urgently. Because of my rare illness.'

Barney thinks about this. He gives me a look that I'm fairly sure is sympathetic.

This is going well.

'Mum and Dad have got my pills,' I say. 'For my rare illness. If I don't take the pills, my rare illness will get worse and I could die.'

Barney thinks about this some more.

'What exactly is this rare illness?' he asks.

Suddenly I realise what he's concerned about. The other kids catching it. And him.

'Don't worry,' I say. 'It doesn't invade other people.'

Barney's eyes are twinkling in the candlelight. He almost looks amused. I feel indignant. People shouldn't be amused by other people's rare illnesses.

'If I don't find Mum and Dad and take those pills in the next two hours,' I say, 'I'll get warts growing inside my tummy and my pee will turn green.'

I stop myself saying any more. I may have gone a bit too far already.

Barney is actually smiling now.

'Zelda's right,' he says. 'You are a good storyteller.'

Poop, I did go too far.

Barney suddenly looks serious.

'She also told me,' he says, 'that you haven't seen your parents for nearly four years.'

I feel myself blushing in the candlelight. What a stupid storytelling mistake. That was as stupid as Father Ludwik telling us Adolf Hitler is a great man.

Desperately I try to think of a way to make the story better. Would Barney believe me if I tell him that I only have to take the pills once every four years?

I don't think so. This is pathetic. I can't tell a decent story to save my life any more. Or Mum and Dad's.

Barney puts his hand on my shoulder and I wait to be escorted back down into the cellar.

But that doesn't happen. Barney hands me the candle, picks up his bag and steers me towards a big rusty door in the wall of the printing factory.

'I'm glad you want to come with me, Felix,' he says.

'Why?' I say, surprised.

Barney suddenly looks very serious.

'I have to confess something,' he says. 'I read one of the stories in your notebook.'

I stare at him, stunned. He just doesn't seem like the sort of person who'd read a private notebook without permission.

'I'm sorry,' he says. 'But I wanted to find out what I could about your parents.'

Before I can say anything about my stories being dumb and not true, Barney grips my shoulder and looks me right in the eyes.

'You're a very good storyteller,' he says.

I don't know what to say.

Before I can think of something, Barney goes on.

'The reason I'm glad you're coming with me, Felix,' he says, 'is because I need your help.'

We pause in the doorway of the printing factory while Barney looks up and down the dark street.

In the moonlight I can see his leather jacket has a small hole in the back. I wonder if it's a bullet hole.

Did Barney get shot once?

Did his family?

Is that why he's looking after other people's kids in a secret cellar?

It might not be a bullet hole. A candle flame could have done it, or a rat. Barney might be a teacher or something. The Nazis might have burnt all the books in his school so he brought some of the kids here to hide them.

'This is the dangerous part,' whispers Barney, still squinting up and down the street. 'If anyone sees us leaving this building, we're sunk.'

Or he could be a sailor.

'Come on,' says Barney. 'All clear. Let's go.'

The streets of the city are filthy, scraps of paper and rubbish everywhere. Some of the buildings have got bits missing from them. The whole place is deserted. I know it's night and everything, but we haven't seen a single person apart from a couple of dead bodies on a street corner.

I manage not to cry.

Barney makes us cross over to the other side, but it's alright, I've already seen they aren't Mum and Dad.

'Where are all the other people?' I say.

'Indoors,' says Barney. 'There's a curfew. That means everybody has to stay indoors after seven at night.'

We go down a narrow laneway with tall apartment buildings on both sides. I can't see a single person through any of the windows. I read once that cities have electric lights, but there doesn't seem to be much electricity going on around here.

Finding Mum and Dad isn't going to be easy, even if I can slip away from Barney while he's concentrating on getting food.

'What happens if people don't do the curfew?' I ask.

'They get shot,' says Barney.

I look at him in alarm. I can tell from his voice he's not joking.

He holds up his leather bag.

'We'll be alright,' he says.

I wonder what's in the bag. Money, maybe. Or something the Nazis need. I hope it's not guns they could use to shoot Jewish booksellers.

I change the subject.

'Why is there a curfew?' I ask.

Dad taught me to use every new word as much as possible after hearing it for the first time.

'This is a ghetto,' says Barney. 'It's a part of the city where the Jews have been sent to live. The Nazis make the rules here.'

I think about this.

Barney knocks on a door, and while we wait he turns to me with a serious expression.

'Felix,' he says. 'You might not be able to find your parents. I know that's a hard thing to hear, but you might not.'

It is a hard thing to hear.

Luckily he's wrong.

'The Jewish people who've been brought to the city,' I say, 'are they all in this ghetto or are there other ghetto curfew places as well?'

Barney doesn't answer.

Perhaps I didn't say the new words right.

A woman leads us into a back room in the apartment. There are several people in the room, all wearing coats and all standing around a bed. The man lying on the bed is wearing a coat too, and holding his head and groaning.

'Lamp, please,' says Barney.

Somebody hands Barney an oil lamp. He bends over the bed and looks into the man's mouth. The man groans even louder.

I glance at the other people. They don't look very well either, though none of them are groaning.

Barney opens his bag and takes out a bundle of metal poles and leather straps. He fits the poles together using little metal wheels to make a kind of robot arm. From his bag he takes the foot pedal from a Singer sewing machine like Mrs Glick used to have. He connects the poles to the pedal with the leather straps.

My imagination is in a frenzy. Is Barney going to show these people how to mend their clothes? Their coats are fairly ragged. Or is this a machine he's invented that helps people grow food in their own homes? There are lots of damp patches on these walls and these people do look very hungry.

After all, this is 1942, so anything's possible.

'Salt water,' says Barney.

While a couple of the people get water from a bucket, Barney attaches a short needle to the end of the robot arm and pedals the sewing machine thing with his foot. The straps make the needle spin round very fast with a loud humming noise.

Suddenly I realise what Barney has just put together.

A dentist's drill.

Barney gives the man in the bed a glass of salty water and a metal bowl.

'Rinse and spit,' he says.

The man does.

I stare in amazement. I take my glasses off and wipe them on my shirt and put them back on.

Barney is a dentist.

Mum went to a dentist once. Me and Dad met him in his waiting room. He was very different to Barney. He was a thin bald man with a squeaky voice who didn't do house calls.

'Felix,' says Barney. 'Over here, please.'

I jolt to attention. Barney wants me to help him. I've never been a dentist's assistant before. Will there be blood?

I squeeze through the people until I'm next to Barney. He's taken the top off the lamp and is holding the tip of the drill in the flame. Heat kills germs, I've read about that.

'Felix,' says Barney as he dips the drill tip into the water the man has spat into the bowl. 'Tell the patient a story, would you?'

The water bubbles as the drill cools. My brain is bubbling too, with confusion.

A story?

Then I get it. When Mum went to the dentist, she had an injection to dull the pain. Barney hasn't given this patient an injection. Times are tough, and there probably aren't enough pain-dulling drugs in ghetto curfew places.

Suddenly my mouth feels dry. I've never told anyone else a story to take their mind off pain. And when I told myself all those stories about Mum and Dad, I wanted to believe them. Plus I didn't have a drill in my mouth.

This is a big responsibility.

'Open wide,' says Barney.

He starts drilling.

'Go on, Felix,' he says.

The groans of the patient and the grinding of the drill and the smell of burning from the patient's mouth make it hard to concentrate but I force myself.

'Once,' I say, 'a boy called William lived in a castle in the mountains and he had a magic carrot.'

The patient isn't looking at Barney any more, he's looking at me.

'If the boy held the carrot right,' I go on, 'he could have three wishes. About anything. Including parents and cakes.'

Barney knocks on another door. A big door at the front of a big building.

'This one will be different,' he says to me. 'But you'll be fine.'

'I hope so,' I say.

My feet blisters are hurting and I'm a bit worried by the Nazi flag flapping over our heads.

Barney puts his hand on my shoulder.

'You did a really good job back there,' he says.

'Poor Mr Grecki was in a lot of pain, but your story helped him get through it. Well done.'

I feel myself glowing, which I haven't done for years, not since the last time I helped Mum and Dad dust the bookshelves and straighten up the folded-down corners of pages.

It's true, Mr Grecki was very grateful. He and his family looked very sad when I asked them if they'd seen Mum and Dad and they said they hadn't.

The door opens.

I nearly faint.

Glaring at us is a Nazi soldier.

Barney says something to him in Nazi language and points to our dentist bag. The soldier nods and we follow him in. As we climb some stairs, Barney whispers to me.

'This patient is German. Tell him a nice story about Germany.'

Suddenly I feel very nervous. I don't know much about Germany. I think I read somewhere that it's completely flat and has a lot of windmills, but I could be wrong.

'I don't speak German,' I mutter to Barney.

'Doesn't matter,' says Barney. 'Say it in Polish and I'll translate.'

The soldier leads us into an upstairs room and I feel even more nervous.

The patient is a Nazi officer. Not the one who did the shooting when we arrived in the city, but he could be a friend of that one. He's sprawled in an armchair holding his face, and when he sees us he scowls and looks like he's blaming us for his toothache.

Barney sets up the drill. He doesn't ask for salt water. I think this is because the Nazi officer is swigging from a bottle. Whatever he's drinking smells very strong. He's doing a lot of rinsing but no spitting.

I don't understand. Why is Barney drilling a Nazi's teeth? And why doesn't the German Nazi army use its own dentists? Perhaps the officers don't like them because they're too rough and they use bayonets instead of drills.

Barney picks up a lamp and looks inside the Nazi officer's mouth.

That's amazing. I've never seen that before. The lamp is connected to a wire. It must be electric.

'Go on, Felix,' says Barney.

He wants me to start. My imagination goes blank. What story can I tell to a Nazi officer in a bad mood? I want to tell a story about how burning books and shooting innocent people makes toothache worse, but I'd better not risk that.

The soldier comes back in with a bulging cloth bag. Poking out the top is a loaf of bread with hardly any mould on it and some turnips and a cabbage.

'Thank you,' says Barney as he starts the drill.

I understand. This is why we're giving this Nazi dental treatment when we could be giving it to a poor Jewish person.

To earn food.

I think of the kids back in the cellar. I didn't tell them a story before, but I can tell one for them now.

'Once,' I say to the Nazi officer, 'two brave German booksellers, I mean soldiers, were hacking their way through the African jungle. Their mission was to reach a remote African village and help mend a, um, windmill.'

Barney translates.

I start making up the most exciting and thrilling story I can, with lots of vicious wild animals and poisonous insects who say nice things about Adolf Hitler.

The Nazi officer seems to be interested. Well, he's not shooting anybody. But he could at any moment.

I try hard to stop my voice wobbling with fear.

I want to do a good job so this patient will be as grateful as the last one was. So that afterwards, when the drilling and the story are over, he'll feel warm and generous towards me.

That's when I'll ask him if he knows where Mum and Dad are.

Once a dentist stopped me from asking a Nazi officer about my parents and I was really mad at him.

I still am, even after a sleep and a long sit on the bucket.

I want to break this stupid toothbrush he made for me into tiny pieces. That's why I'm scrubbing my teeth so hard.

The Nazi officer was smiling by the time I was halfway through the story. By the time I'd described how the two German soldiers turned the windmill into a giant water pump and built a lake for the African kids to go ice skating on, he was laughing. He made me carry on with the story even after Barney finished drilling.

At the end the Nazi officer asked me to write the story down so he could send it home to his kids.

Of course I said yes.

I told him it would be in Polish and it would

take me a couple of days. The Nazi officer didn't mind at all, just asked me to drop it round when it's finished. I don't think he's a friend of the other Nazi officer, the murderer. I think when he hears about what's happened to Mum and Dad he'll want to help them.

But before I could start telling him, Barney grabbed me and the bag of food and we left.

'Too dangerous,' Barney told me in the street, but he wouldn't say why.

This toothbrush is unbreakable. It's only wood and bristles, but Barney must have some dentist's secret of making it really strong.

'Felix,' says a muffled voice.

I look down.

Zelda has joined me at the teeth-cleaning bowl. Her mouth is already foaming with Barney's home-made toothpaste that he makes from chalk dust and soap.

'When you went out with Barney last night,' she says, 'did you find our parents?'

I don't know what to say.

Her eyes are shining hopefully above the foam and suddenly I feel terrible. Here's me moaning about waiting two days to have a conversation with a Nazi officer, and poor Zelda still doesn't even know her parents are dead.

Her face falls.

'You didn't find them?' she says.

I shake my head.

We look at each other. I try and think up a story about how parents aren't really that important, but I can't because they are.

'I know a place we can see them from,' says Zelda.

I smile sadly. At least she's learning how to use her imagination.

'Up there,' she says.

I look up to where she's pointing. A needle of daylight, bigger than the others, is coming in through a crack where one of the walls meets the ceiling.

'Jacob says that from up there he can see outside into the street,' says Zelda.

I sigh. Everyone's a storyteller these days.

'It's true,' says a voice behind me.

Jacob is climbing off his sack bed, blinking very indignantly. Several of the other kids are waking up too.

'It's easy,' says Jacob. 'You make a pile of beds and climb up. I did it last night.'

'He did,' says Zelda. 'But he wouldn't let me.'

I look at them both. I can see they're telling the truth. When people lie, their toothpaste foam droops.

'Let's do it now,' says Zelda excitedly.

I peer over at the other side of the cellar. Barney is still in bed, snoring. When he's been out at night he usually sleeps pretty late.

'Alright,' I say.

It's worth a try. And not just for me. It might be good for Zelda, too. She might see an aunty or uncle or something.

'I can't see my mummy and daddy yet,' says Zelda. 'Can you see yours?'

'Not yet,' I say.

I get a firmer grip with my bare feet on the wobbly pile of beds, hold Zelda's arm tighter so we don't both fall, press my glasses harder against the crack in the wall and try to see something that isn't feet and legs. That's the problem with looking out into the street at ground level, you don't get to see the tops of people.

It's very confusing. I can see hundreds of feet and legs milling around out there. With this many Jewish people in Poland, how come Mum and Dad's shop didn't do better?

'I can see my mummy's feet,' yells Zelda. 'Over there, in her brown shoes.'

'Shhh,' calls Chaya from down below. 'You'll wake Barney.'

'It's alright,' says Jacob, his voice strained from helping Chaya prop up the pile of beds. 'Barney's a heavy sleeper.'

Zelda's eyes are pressed to the crack in the wall.

'Over there,' she squeaks. 'Mummy's feet.'

I know how she feels. I thought I saw Dad's dark green trousers. Until I saw another pair. And then three more.

I try to see if any of the feet and legs look as if they're doing the sort of things that Mum and Dad do, like carrying big piles of books or having discussions about books or reading somebody else's book over their shoulder.

I can't tell. The feet and legs could be doing anything. I can identify those two pairs of legs over there. They belong to two men who are wrestling on the ground over a piece of bread. And those there belong to another man who's just collapsed and is lying on the cobbles while people step over him. But the rest of the feet and legs could belong to anybody. The only thing I can tell for sure is that none of them belong to kids.

I press my nose to the crack in the wall and try and get a whiff of Mum's perfume.

Nothing.

I cram my ear to the crack to try and hear Mum and Dad's voices.

All I can hear is trucks arriving and people yelling. Some of them sound like German soldiers.

Suddenly all the feet and legs are scattering and running away.

'Mummy,' yells Zelda.

She's jiggling up and down. The pile of beds underneath us is toppling.

'Look out,' yells Jacob.

I plummet towards the floor.

Luckily the beds break my fall. So does Jacob. When my head stops spinning and I find my glasses,

I help him out from under a sack. And almost step back into Barney, who is standing there, hands on his hips, glaring at us.

I can't give him my full attention yet, not till I've made sure Zelda is alright. If she landed on this stone floor . . .

Phew, there she is, crawling around on her hands and knees.

'Where are my slippers?' she's saying. 'I need to put my slippers on so I can go and see Mummy.'

I look at how desperately she's searching and suddenly I know I have to tell her. I don't want to, and I don't know how to, but I have to. The poor kid can't go on like this. She needs to know the truth.

'You're sure they were both dead?' says Barney quietly as we watch the other kids put the beds back into position and Zelda put her slippers on.

I nod.

I tell him about the feathers I held under their noses.

'They'd been shot,' I say. 'So had the chickens.'

I try not to think about the blood.

Barney frowns.

'You're right,' he says. 'Zelda does need to know.'

I wait, but he doesn't say anything else.

'Will you tell her?' I say.

Barney frowns some more.

'I think it's better if you do it,' he says. 'You've both been through a lot together and she trusts you. And you were there.'

That's what I've been dreading he'd say.

'I don't know how to,' I say quietly.

Barney looks at me. I haven't noticed before how red his eyes are. Must be because he works at night a lot.

'Just tell her the story of what you saw,' he says. 'You don't have to make anything up.'

'Alright,' I say.

I wish I could make things up for Zelda. I wish I could tell her a happy story. About how my glasses were affected by the heat of the fire, and how her parents aren't really dead, and how they're just having a holiday on a desert island with a cake shop, and how they'll be coming back for her as soon as their suntans are completed.

But I can't.

I tell Zelda the story of what I saw.

She doesn't believe me.

'No,' she yells, throwing herself onto her sack.

Barney puts his hand gently on her shoulder. The other kids watch silently, their faces sad.

I tell her again, still without making anything up.

This time she doesn't yell. For a long time her body shakes in Barney's arms without any sound at all.

I'm trembling myself, partly at the memory of what I saw, and partly because, for Zelda, my story has made her parents dead.

Now several of the other kids are crying too.

Ruth stops brushing her hair and lets her tears run down her face.

'Once,' she whispers, 'some goblins hit my dad with sticks. They hit him with sticks till he died.'

Barney reaches over and squeezes her hand.

Jacob is sobbing too.

'Nana was burned,' he says, tears trickling through his blinks. 'I got home from school and they were all burned. Nana and Popi and Elie and Martha and Olek.'

Henryk stands up and kicks his bed.

'I hate goblins,' he says. 'They killed Sigi and cut his tail off.'

Chaya puts her good arm round him and holds him while he sobs. She lowers her gentle face and speaks quietly.

'Once a princess lived in a castle. It was a small castle, but the princess loved it, and she loved her family who lived there with her. Then one day the evil goblins came looking for information about their enemies. They thought the princess knew the information, but she didn't. To make her tell, the goblins gave the princess three wishes. Either they could hurt her, or they could hurt the old people, or they could hurt the babies.'

Chaya pauses, trembling, staring at the floor. I can see how hard it is for her to finish her story.

'The princess chose the first wish,' she says quietly. 'But because she didn't know any information, the goblins made all three wishes come true.'

We're all crying now. Moshe is still chewing his wood, but tears are running down his face too.

A whole cellar full of tears.

I take Chaya's hand for a while. Then I go over and Barney lets me hug Zelda. I can feel the sadness shaking her whole body.

All around me poor kids are crying for their dead families.

My tears are different.

I feel so lucky because somewhere out there I know my mum and dad are still alive.

Once I told Zelda a story that made her cry, so I lay on her sack with her for hours and hours until she fell asleep. Then I started writing down the African story for the Nazi officer until I fell asleep too.

Now Barney is shaking me.

'Felix,' he whispers. 'We've run out of water. I need you to help me find some.'

I sit up and put my notebook inside my shirt. I reach for my shoes and the rags to pack around my feet.

'Try these,' says Barney.

He hands me a pair of boots. I stare at them in the candlelight.

They're almost new. I've never had an almost new pair of boots before. When I was little Mum and Dad used to get my shoes from other families with bigger kids who liked reading.

I put the boots on.

They fit.

'Thanks,' I say. 'Where did you get them?'

I can see Barney doesn't want to tell me. I remember something he once said.

'You don't have to make anything up,' I add.

Barney smiles.

'I bought them,' he says. 'Three turnips.'

I stare at him, horrified. Three turnips is a fortune. We could have made soup for all of us with three turnips.

'Water hunters need good shoes for running,' says Barney. 'In case the water tries to get away.'

I look down at Barney's shoes. They're both split open and wound round with rope.

Barney sees me looking.

'Alright,' he says quietly. 'I'll tell you the truth. I got you the boots because everybody deserves to have something good in their life at least once.'

I don't know what to say. That is one of the kindest things I've ever heard, including in stories.

'Thanks,' I whisper. 'But . . .'

I'm confused. Surely Barney knows I've got lots of other good things in my life. More than anyone else in this cellar, probably.

Barney locks the trapdoor and I follow him through the dark printing factory, an empty bucket in each hand, my feet snug and grateful in my new boots.

As we get close to the big rusty door, Barney

suddenly blows out the candle and puts his finger on my lips.

I can hear it too. Voices and footsteps out in the street.

It's after curfew time. Everybody's meant to be indoors.

We creep over to a window. Barney rubs a small patch on the dusty glass and we peep out.

The street is crowded with people, all trudging in the moonlight, all in the same direction. Jewish people, I can tell by the armbands on their coats. Some are carrying bags and bundles. They're so close I can hear their voices, even through the glass.

'Yes, but where?' says a woman wearing a scarf.

A man with his arm round her rolls his eyes. He looks like he's done it before, so he's probably her husband.

'I don't know exactly,' he says. 'The countryside. Does it matter where? For each day's work we get a loaf of bread and sausage and marmalade. That's all that matters.'

The husband and wife are too far away now and I can't hear them any more because their voices are mixed up with all the others.

A man with a loud voice is passing the window.

'Please,' he's saying. 'Which is it? Russia? Romania? Hungary? You must know where we're going.'

I shrink back. The person he's talking to is a Nazi soldier.

'Countryside,' says the soldier. 'Beautiful. Much food. Easy work.'

I look at Barney, to see if he's thinking what I'm thinking.

The Nazis are taking the Jewish people to the countryside to work. Farming, perhaps, or looking after sheep. Anything to get their minds off books, probably.

That means Mum and Dad will be going there.

'Barney,' I whisper. 'Can we go too? Zelda and Henryk and all of us?'

Barney looks as though this is the worst idea anybody has ever had in the history of the world.

'No,' he says.

'But it could be great,' I say. 'A farmer could let us live in his barn and we could make cheese and sell it.'

Barney isn't even listening, just peering out of the window.

The street outside is empty now. I can hear the last of the Jewish people and the Nazi soldiers fading into the distance.

'Come on,' says Barney, unchaining the big door. 'We've got water to find. Let's go.'

In the cool night air my thoughts are clear.

I don't say anything more about the countryside. I know what I'm going to do. Once me and Barney have found some water and got it back to the cellar, I'm going to finish writing my African story and give it to the Nazi officer and ask him which bit of the countryside Mum and Dad have been taken to.

Then I'm going to wake Zelda up and we'll go there on our own.

I don't believe it.

Barney just walked into an apartment without knocking. He just looked around the stairwell to make sure nobody was watching, pushed the door open and barged in.

Lucky the stairwell was deserted.

'Is this your apartment?' I ask him.

'No,' he says. He's saying that a lot tonight.

He stops in the hallway. His shoulders slump. I see what's caught his eye. On the floor is a Jewish candlestick, the type that holds a row of candles. It's completely squashed, as if somebody's stamped on it.

'This place belongs to friends of mine,' says Barney quietly.

I understand. They must have gone to work in the countryside and forgotten to lock up.

I follow Barney into a room. It's an unusual sort of room. I need a moment to take it all in.

The big leather chair.

The two sinks.

The robot-arm drill.

Now I understand. It's a dentist's surgery.

'See if the water's on,' says Barney.

I don't waste time. I take my buckets over to one of the sinks and turn the tap. Nothing.

'It's off,' I say.

Barney is rummaging in cupboards and stuffing things into his pockets. Metal syringes. Packets of needles. Small bottles filled with liquid.

'That's not water, is it?' I say, puzzled.

Barney looks at me and I get the feeling he wishes I hadn't seen what he's doing.

'It's a drug,' he says. 'Dentists use it to stop their patients feeling pain.'

'I know,' I say. 'My mum had it once.'

Barney comes over and crouches down so his face is level with mine.

'I don't want you or any of the others to touch this,' he says, holding up one of the little bottles. 'It's very dangerous. Only dentists should touch it.'

'Why is it dangerous?' I ask.

'If a person takes too much,' says Barney, 'they go into a very deep sleep and never wake up.'

Something about the way he says it makes me shiver. But at least his patients will have something else to dull their pain when I'm in the countryside with Mum and Dad and Zelda and can't tell them stories.

I remember why we're here.

'I'll look in the other rooms for water,' I say.

'There's a bathroom down the hall,' says Barney.

We go into the bathroom and straight away I can see we're in luck. The bath is full of water. I scoop some out with one of my buckets.

'Hang on,' says Barney, taking the bucket from me and tipping the water back. 'Somebody's had a bath in that. It's dirty. Better not risk it.'

I stare at the water, confused.

That's not dirty. It's just a bit soapy with a few hairs in it. One person's been in that, two tops. If Barney wants to see dirty water he should go to an orphanage on bath night. There's not even any grit in this as far as I can see.

'See if there's any food in the kitchen,' says Barney. 'I'll fill the buckets from this.'

He's lifting the lid off the toilet cistern. Which I have to admit is a good idea. Two buckets of clean water at least.

I go down the hall to the kitchen, wondering why there are cooking utensils on the hall floor.

In the kitchen things are even worse. The floor is covered with broken plates and bits of cooked food. I crouch down, wondering if Barney is going to be fussy about food that's been on the floor.

Then I realise there's someone else in the room. Oh.

It's a little kid, about two, in a high chair.

I can't tell if it's a girl or a boy because there's too much blood on the little body.

Oh.

I scream for Barney.

He comes running in and he almost falls over himself when he sees the poor horrible sight but then he grabs me and drags me out into the hall.

'It's a little kid,' I sob. 'They shouldn't shoot little kids.'

'Shhhh,' says Barney. He sounds like he's sobbing too. He pushes my face into his coat.

'Why didn't the parents do something?' I sob. 'Why didn't they take their kid to the countryside?'

Barney is shaking. He hugs me very hard.

'Sometimes,' he says, his voice shaking as well, 'parents can't protect their kids even though they love them more than anything in the world. Sometimes, even when they try their very hardest, they can't save them.'

I can feel Barney's tears falling onto me. For a while he doesn't say anything, just strokes my head.

I stroke his hand.

Something tells me he needs it too.

'Your mum and dad loved you, Felix,' says Barney. 'They did everything they could to protect you.'

Loved? Why is he saying that as if it's in the past?

'I'm going to find them,' I say. 'I'm going to live in the countryside with them.'

I feel Barney give a big painful sigh.

'There is no countryside,' he says quietly. 'The Nazis aren't taking anyone to the countryside. They're taking Jews away to kill them.'

I stare up at him.

What?

That's the stupidest story I've ever heard. Didn't he hear what the Nazi soldier said to the Jewish people outside the window?

I kick and struggle to get myself out of his grip so I can go and find Mum and Dad before the Nazis take them to the countryside. But Barney is holding me too tight. His arms are too strong. I can't get away.

'It's true, Felix,' he says. His voice sounds like he's at a funeral.

'How do you know?' I yell at him.

'Somebody escaped from one of the death camps,' he says. 'This man came to the ghetto to try and warn the rest of us.'

My head is hurting.

Death camps?

'You're making this up,' I yell at Barney. 'If it was true, you would have warned the people leaving tonight.'

I feel his chest heaving for a long time before he answers.

'They wouldn't have believed me,' he says. 'They didn't believe the man from the death camp. Not even after the Nazis killed him. And I need to be alive so I can take care of you and the others.'

It's on Barney's face, I can see it.

He's telling the truth.

Oh Mum.

Oh Dad.

My imagination goes into a frenzy, trying to think up ways for them to escape, places for them to hide, reasons why none of this has happened to them.

Every time I start to think of something I remember the poor little kid in the kitchen.

Barney is still holding me tight and I can feel the metal syringes in his coat pocket pressing against my cheek.

Suddenly I want him to stick one of the syringes into me so I can go into a deep sleep and never wake up and never feel this bad ever again.

Once I loved stories and now I hate them.

I hate stories about God and Jesus and Mary and that crowd and how they're meant to be taking care of us.

I hate stories about the beautiful countryside with much food and easy work.

I hate stories about parents who say they'll come back for their children and never do.

I roll over on my bed. I push my face into my sack so I can't hear Barney over at the other side of the cellar, reading some stupid story to the others. I never want to hear another story. I never want to write another story. I never want to read another book. What good have books ever done me and Mum and Dad? We'd have been better off with guns.

'Felix,' says a faint voice in my ear.

It's Zelda.

I ignore her.

'Are your parents dead too?' she asks.

I don't answer.

I feel her put something round my neck. It's her silver chain with the little heart on it.

'This is to make you feel better,' she says.

I don't want to feel better.

I don't want to feel anything.

I just want to be like the Nazi officer, the murderer one. Cold and hard and bored with people.

Zelda strokes my head.

I try to ignore that too. But I can't. There's something wrong.

Her hand is hot.

Very hot.

I sit up and look at her. Her face is pale. But when I touch her cheek, her skin is burning.

'I've got a temperature,' she whispers. 'Don't you know anything?'

Then her eyes go funny and she flops down onto the floor.

'Barney, quick,' I yell, my voice squeaky with panic. 'Zelda's sick.'

'I don't like you going out alone,' says Barney.

I can see he doesn't. I've never seen him look so worried. All day while we took it in turns to wipe Zelda's hot skin with wet rags, Barney was telling us she was going to be alright. But ever since the other kids got exhausted and went to bed, he's been looking more and more worried.

'Chaya can't run with her bad arm,' he says. 'Jacob and Ruth and Moshe get too scared outside, and the others are too young.'

'I'll be alright on my own,' I say.

'I can't leave Zelda like this,' says Barney, dipping the rag into the bucket of water and pressing it gently to her face. 'But she needs aspirin. If we can't get her temperature down in the next few hours . . .'

He stops because Zelda's eyes flutter open.

'I'm hot,' she croaks.

I lift her cup to her white lips and she swallows a little.

'There'll be aspirin in the dental surgery we were in last night,' says Barney.

I don't say anything.

I try not to think of what's in the kitchen of that apartment.

'But if you don't want to go back there,' Barney says, 'you'll find empty apartments in most of the buildings. And you'll almost certainly find aspirin in one of them. In a bathroom or kitchen or bedside drawer.'

I nod. I know about aspirin. Mother Minka used to get headaches from praying too much.

'Are you sure you can do this?' asks Barney.

'Yes,' I say.

I know what Barney was going to say before Zelda opened her eyes. If we can't get her temperature down in the next few hours, she'll die.

I must find her some aspirin.

And there's something else I must bring back for her as well.

I slip quietly out of our building without anybody seeing me.

The ghetto streets are different tonight.

They're just as dark and scary and full of litter as always, but not so deserted. Nazi trucks are zooming around. German soldiers are running in and out of apartment blocks. In the distance I can hear shooting.

I creep into an empty apartment.

No asprin.

I try next door.

Yes. A whole jar.

But I haven't finished yet. There's something else I need to find.

All the apartments in this block seem to be empty. I can hear Nazis down the street but I haven't seen a single Jewish person.

I creep down yet another apartment hallway, holding the candle out in front of me so I don't trip over any of the toys or ornaments or smashed photos on the floor.

More gunshots in the distance.

This will have to be the last apartment. If I don't find it here, I'll have to give up.

I close my eyes as I step into the kitchen. I open them slowly. After last night I won't ever be able to go into a kitchen with my eyes open again.

This one's alright, except for a big dark stain on the floor that could be just gravy.

I ignore it and start opening cupboards.

Nothing in the top ones.

I bend down and start opening the bottom ones. Zelda's locket chain keeps getting caught on the cupboard doors. I toss it over my shoulder so it hangs down my back.

Two cupboards left.

Please God, Jesus, Mary and the Pope, if you're still on our side please let this be the one.

Yes.

There, lying next to a mouldy potato, something that will help Zelda just as much as the aspirin.

A carrot.

I know I should get out of this apartment as fast as I can. I know I should sprint down the stairs into the street and hurry along the darkest back alleys to the cellar so Zelda can have her aspirin and her carrot soup.

But I can't just yet.

Not now I've seen this bedroom.

It's exactly like the room I used to have at home.

The wallpaper is the same, the reading lamp is the same, the bookshelves are the same. The one thing that's different is that there are six beds crammed in here.

These kids have even got some of the same books.

I clamber over the beds and squeeze onto the

floor and take a book from the shelf. *Just William* by Richmal Crompton. It's still one of my favourite books in the whole world. And probably one of Dodie's by now. As I open it I try not to remember Mum and Dad reading it to me.

Instead, I read a bit to myself. About William's dog. He's called Jumble and he's a mixture of about a hundred different dogs and William loves him even when he pees in William's new boots.

Mum and Dad said I can have a dog like Jumble one day.

Stop it.

Stop thinking about them.

William is training Jumble to be a pirate. That's what I love about William. He always stays hopeful, and no matter how bad things get, no matter how much his world turns upside down, his mum and dad never die.

Not ever.

I know I should be getting back, but I can't get up at the moment. All I can do is stay here on the floor, with *Just William* and Zelda's carrot, thinking about Mum and Dad and crying.

What's that noise?

It's dark. The candle must have burnt down. Oh no, I must have fallen asleep here on the floor.

The noise again, thumping. A dog growling.

Jumble?

No, there's somebody in the apartment.

Several people. Boots thumping. Torches flashing. Men shouting in another language.

Nazi soldiers.

Where can I hide?

Under the beds. No, every story I've ever read where somebody hides under a bed they get caught.

I know. Under the books.

I lie next to the bookcase and tilt it forward so all the books slide off the shelves and onto me. With one hand I arrange books over all the bits of me that feel uncovered. It's not easy in the dark. I pray to Richmal Crompton that I haven't missed any bits. Then I slide my hand under the pile and stay very still.

Bang.

The bedroom door is kicked open.

Torchlight stabs between the books.

I hold my breath. I can hear someone else breathing. Then footsteps, leaving the room.

I wait.

More banging and shouting in other rooms. Dogs barking. Getting further away. I think they've gone.

I wait more.

I can't hear them at all.

I scramble out from under the books. I strike a match and find *Just William* for Zelda and the others. Then I run. Down the hall. Out into the stairwell. Down the stairs. Skidding on the clothes and shoes that have been chucked around everywhere.

Jumping over the cooking pots. And the musical instruments.

Oh no, I've tripped.

I'm falling.

Ow.

Quick, get up. I don't think I'm hurt. I've got my glasses. The carrot and the asprin are safe in my pocket. *Just William* is still in my hand.

That wasn't as bad as it could have been. Except for the torchlight that's suddenly dazzling me from the doorway of one of the ground floor apartments.

It's a Nazi soldier.

He's yelling at me. He's got a pile of clothes and stuff in a box clutched to his chest. He's aiming his torch at me and coming closer.

I put my hands up to show I'm not armed.

The soldier tucks his torch under his chin.

Why does he need a spare hand?

For his gun?

No, to grab *Just William* from me. He stares at it, frowning. He puts it in his box. Now he's staring at something else. On my chest. Zelda's locket, which is smashed and hanging off the chain in two halves. He peers at it, breathing smelly drink fumes out of his hairy nostrils.

Then he lets go of it and turns and sticks his head back into the apartment and starts yelling. I think he's calling to someone else. A William fan, maybe.

I don't wait to find out.

The gate to the back alley is open. I fling myself through it and run down the alley and into the next one, weaving from alley to alley, not stopping, going for the narrowest ones I can find, the ones not wide enough for a tank to squeeze down, or a troop carrier, or a Nazi soldier loaded up with stuff he's been looting.

I only stop when I suddenly find myself in a wide street, bright with moonlight, empty and silent.

I crouch down next to a wall, gasping for breath, and have a look at Zelda's locket to see what the soldier found so interesting.

One half of the locket is empty.

In the other half is a tiny photograph. A man and a woman standing in front of a Polish flag. Zelda's parents, they must be. Her poor dead parents. The woman has hair a bit like Zelda's, only shorter, and a face a bit like Zelda's, only older.

I rub some Nazi finger grease off the photo and see Zelda's father more clearly and the clothes he's wearing and I almost stop breathing even though I'm still desperate for air.

Zelda's father is wearing a uniform.

A Nazi uniform.

Thank you God, Jesus, Mary, the Pope and Richmal Crompton. I thought I was never going to find my way back, but I know where I am now.

This is the street next to where our cellar is.

If I can get past that corner without any Nazi patrols coming along, I'll be in our cellar in no time and Zelda can have her carrot soup and aspirin.

I know what you're thinking, God and Richmal and all the others. If Zelda's dad's a Nazi, does she deserve carrot soup and aspirin?

Yes.

She can't help what her father did. Plus he's dead now and so's her mum and I don't know if she's got any other living relatives but after what we've been through together that makes me one and I say yes.

Oh no. I can hear trucks. And soldiers shouting. And dogs barking.

Where are they?

I look around desperately.

They're not in this street.

I crouch by the building on the corner and peer into our street.

Oh.

The trucks are parked in front of our building.

Oh.

Nazi soldiers are aiming guns at the printing factory doorway. Dogs are straining on leads and snarling. Not dogs like Jumble. These are all dogs with only one type of dog in them.

Killers.

Somebody must have tipped the Nazis off. A disgruntled dental patient probably.

How can I warn Barney and the others? How can

I get in there without being seen and help Barney find a secret way out that the Nazis don't know about and get the kids out in disguise if necessary and . . .

Too late.

I can hear other soldiers shouting and other dogs barking, inside the printing factory.

I can hear kids screaming.

It doesn't matter any more who sees me.

I run towards the cellar.

Once the Nazis found our cellar. They dragged us all out and made us walk through the ghetto while they pointed guns at us.

'Barney,' I whisper. 'Where are they taking us?'

Barney doesn't answer for a while. I know why. He's got little Janek on his chest and Henryk holding his hand and the other kids huddled around him and some of them are close to tears and he doesn't want to upset them any more. Ruth has lost her hairbrush. The Nazis wouldn't let Jacob bring his teddy bear. At least Moshe has still got his piece of wood to chew.

'We're going to the railway station,' says Barney at last.

'Will there be water there for Zelda?' I ask.

'Yes,' he says.

I hope he's right. She's on my back, hot and limp, and dawn's just starting, and if we can't give her the aspirin soon she's going to burn up.

'Is the station far?' I ask Barney.

'Cheer up everyone,' says Barney, ignoring me. 'It's a beautiful summer day. We're going on an outing. Let's all enjoy it. Has everyone got their toothbrush?'

The other kids all hold up their toothbrushes.

The Nazi soldiers are staring. They probably haven't seen unbreakable toothbrushes before.

'I've lost my toothbrush,' whispers Zelda in my ear.

'It's OK,' I say. 'You can borrow mine.'

This makes me extra glad I was able to get into the cellar and grab Zelda and my stuff before the Nazis dragged me back out. Even though Zelda is pretty heavy and I think the station probably is a long way. When grown-ups go cheerful on a trip it means you won't be getting there for ages.

It can also mean when you do get there you'll be killed.

I tilt my head back and give Zelda a kiss on the cheek so she won't know I'm having scary thoughts.

One thing is puzzling me.

If the Nazis are going to kill us, why didn't they shoot us in the cellar? It would have been much easier for them. Now they have to march us through the streets in the hot sun. They look really grumpy in their thick uniforms.

I get it.

They must want other people to see us. Other

Jewish people hiding in the buildings along these streets. Peeping out and seeing us and knowing it's hopeless and deciding they might as well give themselves up.

I straighten up and try not to look hopeless.

You know how when things are really bad and you feel like curling up and hiding but instead you take deep breaths and the air reaches your brain and helps you think better?

That's happening to me.

I've just thought of a way of saving Zelda's life.

'Zelda,' I whisper. 'Can you see I'm wearing your locket round my neck?'

'Yes,' she says.

'I want you to take it off me and put it on you,' I say.

She doesn't touch it.

'I gave it to you,' she says.

'Please,' I say. 'This is very important.'

She hesitates.

'It's a lovely gift,' I say. 'It makes me feel not quite so bad about my mum and dad. But now I want to give it back to you. Please let me.'

Zelda hesitates some more. Then I feel her hot little fingers reaching for the chain.

The railway yard is crowded with Jewish people standing and sitting in queues, waiting to get onto a train that stretches so far along the track I can't see the front of it or the back.

'Wow,' says Henryk. 'I've never been on a train before.'

Several of the other kids say they haven't either.

'We'll all be going on it soon,' says Barney. 'Who's excited?'

The kids all say they are, except for Moshe who just chews his wood and Zelda who just clings to my neck.

I'm glad the other kids are excited because it means they haven't seen what I can see now that I've wiped my glasses.

Nazi soldiers with dogs are pushing people onto the train really roughly. It's not a normal sort of train. The carriages are like big boxes with sliding doors. Some people don't want to get on and the Nazi soldiers are hitting them with sticks and whips.

Halfway along our queue a woman collapses onto the ground.

A Nazi soldier steps over to her and shoots her.

Oh.

'No,' screams Ruth.

'Make a tent,' says Barney. 'Everyone make a tent.'

Chaya and Jacob and Barney take their coats off and we all huddle together and the others put their arms into the air and Barney throws the coats over us.

I can't put my arms up because I'm holding Zelda on my back.

Barney reaches into his coat pocket above our heads and takes out the water bottle Mr Kopek gave me. It's been filled again. Barney passes it to the others.

'Just one sip each,' he says. 'Felix, did you get the aspirin?'

I nod.

Barney takes Zelda into his arms.

'Crush two into powder,' he says.

I grind the aspirin into my palm with my thumb. Barney makes sure each person only has a small sip of water and that there's some left in the bottle.

'Put the powder into the water and shake it up,' he tells me.

I do. I hand the bottle to Barney. He puts it to Zelda's lips.

'This won't taste nice,' he says. 'But you must drink it.'

She does, screwing up her face.

While she's busy drinking, I huddle closer to Barney.

'Look at this,' I say.

I show him the locket round Zelda's neck. He stares at the photo of her parents. Even in the hot gloom of our tent I can see he knows what it means. Chaya does too.

'I hate Polish people who join the Nazis,' she mutters.

Barney sighs. 'The Polish resistance must have killed them,' he says softly.

I don't know what resistance means, but this isn't the time to learn new words. There's something much more urgent we need to do.

'We must tell someone,' I say.

Barney nods.

'Stay in the tent,' he says to the others. 'We'll be back soon.'

Barney and Zelda and me crawl out of the tent.

I squint around the railway yard, looking for someone to tell, someone who can save Zelda.

Suddenly I see him.

Thank you God, Jesus, Mary, the Pope and Richmal Crompton, you are on our side after all.

It's the Nazi officer who was the dental patient. The one who wants my African story for his kids. I pull my notebook from my shirt and rip out the pages with the African story on it. It's only half finished, but these are tough times and I'm sure he'll understand.

I start to go over to him.

Barney grabs me. 'If you leave a queue in a place like this,' he says, 'you get shot.'

'Sorry,' I say.

That was stupid, I wasn't thinking.

'Excuse me,' I yell at the Nazi officer, waving the pages. 'I've got your story. Over here.'

He doesn't hear me at first, but I shout some more until Barney stops me, and when a soldier comes over and starts yelling at me even louder and pointing his gun at my head, the officer looks up and sees the pages I'm waving and comes over himself.

He orders the soldier away.

'Here it is,' I say. 'The story you wanted.'

I hold the pages out to him. He takes them, looks at them, smiles, folds them up and puts them in his pocket.

'Also,' I say, 'there's something else.'

I point to the locket hanging round Zelda's neck.

Barney puts his hand on my arm. I remember the Nazi officer doesn't speak Polish.

The officer is staring at the locket. Barney lifts it up so he can see it better and starts speaking to him in German.

'That's my mummy and daddy,' says Zelda quietly to the Nazi officer. 'They're dead. The Polish assistance killed them.'

The Nazi officer looks at the photo for a long time. Then he looks at Zelda and at Barney and at me and at the tent.

He points to Zelda and Barney and then points to the railway yard gate.

Yes.

He's saying they can go.

Barney speaks to him some more in German, pointing to me and the other kids, who are peering out of the tent. He must be asking if we can go too.

The Nazi officer shakes his head. He points to Zelda and Barney again.

'Go with Zelda,' I say to Barney.

He ignores me. He says more things to the Nazi officer. I don't speak German, but I can tell he's pleading.

The Nazi officer shakes his head again. He's starting to look angry.

'Go with Zelda,' I beg Barney. 'I'll look after the others.'

The other kids start screaming. Nazi soldiers have grabbed them and are dragging them towards the train. One starts dragging me.

As I'm being lifted up I see Barney push Zelda's hand into the Nazi officer's hand. Barney comes running after us, yelling at the soldiers to leave us alone. Zelda struggles to get away from the Nazi officer, kicking and screaming.

'Felix,' she yells, 'Wait.'

Now I can't see her. I'm in one of the train boxcars, lying on the floor and on other people. I grab my glasses. Henryk lands on top of me. Other kids as well. Ruth is crying. Chaya is holding her bad arm. Jacob is holding little Janek to his chest. Other people are being thrown on top of us.

Through the tangle of people I see Barney climbing into the boxcar, crawling towards us, asking if we're alright.

'Zelda,' I yell, hoping she can hear me in the total confusion. 'Goodbye.'

But it's not goodbye. A soldier throws Zelda into the boxcar on top of us. Then he slides the door closed with a crash.

'Zelda,' I moan. 'Why didn't you stay?'

'I bit the Nazi,' she says. 'Don't you know anything?'

I put my arm round Zelda and we lie here shivering.

Outside people are screaming and dogs are barking and soldiers are shouting but the loudest noises are the gunshots.

Bang. Bang. Bang.

Suddenly I realise they're not gunshots. I realise what the soldiers are doing. They're nailing the train door shut.

Once I went on my first train journey, but I wouldn't call it exciting, I'd call it painful and miserable.

There are so many of us in this boxcar that most of us have to stand up. Every time the train lurches, we lurch too and squash each other.

'Sorry,' I say each time to the people around me.

At least the little kids have got a space to sit down. Not all the people wanted to make room at first, because it meant the rest of us were more squashed, but Barney had a word to them and then they did.

'Sorry.'

Barney's got all the kids doing a lice hunt, which is a really good idea. We're packed in so tight here we could be giving each other lice without knowing it. Plus nothing passes the time on a long journey like a lice hunt.

Zelda isn't doing it, she's asleep.

Please God and the others, let her get better.

'Sorry.'

I try and make myself thinner to give some of the old people more space. It must be terrible for them. I'm young and I'm used to going without food and water and space.

'Sorry.'

'For God's sake,' yells a man near me. 'Stop saying sorry.'

Barney gives the man a long look.

'He's just a kid,' says Barney. 'Give him a break.'

The man looks like he's going to explode.

'A break?' he says. 'A break? Who's giving us a break?'

I know how the man feels. We've been travelling for hours and this train hasn't stopped once for a toilet break. People can't hold it in for ever, which is why we've had to start going in the corner of the carriage.

Well, Ruth and Moshe and three of the other people have. Everyone else is desperately trying to hold it in because there isn't any toilet paper.

'Are we there yet?' says Henryk, looking up from Ruth's hair.

'Be patient,' says Barney softly. 'Don't let those lice get away.'

'Will we be there soon?' says Jacob, looking up from little Janek's wispy hair and blinking hopefully.

'Shhhh,' says Barney.

I know what he's worried about. People who hate 'sorry' probably hate 'are we there yet' just as much. Specially people who are trying not to think about two other words.

The two that Barney used once.

Death camp.

'Sorry,' says an elderly woman as she struggles through the rest of us to the toilet corner. 'Sorry, I have to.'

We all turn away, those of us that can, to give her some privacy.

Poor woman.

Having no toilet paper isn't so bad when you're young and you've lived in an orphanage a long way from the shops and you're used to sometimes just letting poo dry on you and then getting on with things. But for older people who are used to tradition it must be awful.

I start thinking about poor Mum and Dad and whether they had to go without toilet paper when they made this trip.

I don't want to think about them making this trip. About them arriving and getting off the train and . . .

Please, I beg my imagination. Give me something else to think about. I can't help Barney look after the kids if I'm a weeping wreck.

Suddenly an idea hits me.

Of course.

I reach into my shirt and after a struggle because a couple of other people's elbows are in my chest I manage to pull out my notebook and rip out a couple of blank pages.

'Here,' I say to the woman in the corner. 'Use this.'

The other people pass it over to her and when she sees what it is she starts crying.

'It's alright,' I say, 'I haven't written on it.'

Barney squeezes my arm.

'Well done, Felix,' he says.

Lots of other people hold their hands out for toilet paper and I rip pages out for them as well. Now I've only got pages left with stories on them. Stories I wrote about Mum and Dad.

I look over at the people crouching in the corner, at the relief on their faces.

Mum and Dad would understand.

I rip the rest of the pages out of my notebook and wriggle past everyone to the toilet corner. I grab a metal bolt poking out of a plank in the wall. If I push the bolt through the pages, they'll hang there and people can tear off a page or two as they need them.

The bolt comes away in my hands.

The wooden plank is rotten.

I kick at it and part of my foot goes through.

'Barney,' I yell.

People are looking at what I've done. A couple of

144

men pull my foot out of the plank and start kicking at the wood themselves. Their big boots make a much bigger hole.

Barney and the men pull at the side of the hole with their hands and more bolts fly out of the wood and suddenly the whole plank comes away.

I can see green countryside speeding past.

One of the men tries to squeeze through.

'Wait,' says Barney. 'We need to make the hole bigger. If you roll out you'll fall on the track. You need to be able to jump clear.'

Everyone squashes back to give Barney and the men more room. Barney jams the plank into the hole and the men push till their faces are bulging.

A second plank splinters and the men kick it out.

They do the same with a third.

'That's enough,' yells one of the men. He takes a couple of steps back and dives out through the hole. The second man follows him.

'Come on,' yells someone else. 'We're free.'

More people fling themselves through the hole.

I grab Barney.

'Won't the Nazis stop the train and catch them?' I say.

Barney shakes his head. 'They won't let anything interfere with their timetable,' he says. 'They don't need to.'

We all freeze, startled, as gunshots echo through the train.

145

Lots of gunshots.

'They've got machine guns on the roof,' says Barney, hugging the little kids to him. 'Easier for them than stopping the train.'

People are peering out of the hole, trying to see what happened to the ones who jumped.

'Look,' screams a woman. 'Some of them have made it. They're running into the woods. They're free.'

I grab Barney again.

'We've got to risk it,' I say.

I can see Barney doesn't agree. I can see why. Henryk and Janek are in tears. Ruth and Jacob are clinging to each other, terrified. Moshe has stopped chewing his wood.

I crouch down and in as calm a voice as I can, I tell them a story. It's a story about some kids who jump off a train and land in a soft meadow and a farmer comes and takes them home and they live happily on the farm with his family and get very good at growing vegetables and in the year 1972 they invent a carrot that cures all illnesses.

I pull Zelda's carrot out of my pocket to show them it's possible.

But I can see that most of them aren't convinced.

'Felix,' says Barney. 'If you want to risk it, I won't stop you. But I have to stay with the ones who don't want to.'

'No,' I say, pleading. 'We all have to jump.'

146

'I don't want to,' says Ruth, clinging to Barney.

'I don't want to,' says Jacob.

'I don't want to,' says Henryk.

'I don't want to,' says Janek.

It's no good. I know I'm not going to change their minds. You can't force people to believe a story. And I can see Barney isn't going to try. Some people would make kids risk machine gun bullets and broken necks when they don't want to, but not Barney.

'I want to,' says a voice, and a warm hand squeezes mine.

It's Zelda.

'Are you sure?' says Barney, feeling her forehead.

'Yes,' says Zelda.

'You're sick,' says Ruth.

'I'm better,' says Zelda.

Barney looks like he's not sure.

'She wants to risk it, Barney,' I say.

'See,' says Zelda. 'Felix knows.'

Chaya hands little Janek to Barney.

'I want to risk it too,' she says.

Barney looks at her for a moment.

'Alright,' he says quietly. 'Anyone else?'

The rest of the kids shake their heads.

I check that Mum and Dad's letters are safely inside my shirt. And my toothbrush. Then I hug Ruth and Jacob and Henryk and Janek and Moshe.

And Barney. Now I've got my arms round him, I don't ever want to let go.

But I have to.

'If you see my mum and dad,' I say, 'will you tell them I love them and that I know they did their very best?'

'Yes,' says Barney.

His eyes are as wet as mine.

'Thank you,' I say.

I touch his beard for a moment and behind us I can hear some of the other people in the boxcar crying.

Barney hugs Zelda and Chaya. They hug the other kids.

'Only two wishes this time,' I say to the ones who are staying. 'But at least we got to choose.'

Moshe, chewing again, smiles sadly.

I take hold of Zelda with one hand and Chaya with the other, and we jump.

Once I lay in a field somewhere in Poland, not sure if I'm alive or dead.

You know how when you jump off a moving train and Nazis shoot at you with machine guns and you see sharp tree stumps coming at you and then you hit the ground so hard you feel like you've smashed your head open and bullets have gone through your chest and you don't survive even though you prayed to God, Jesus, Mary, the Pope and Richmal Crompton?

That's what's happened to poor Chaya.

She's lying next to me on the grass, bleeding and not breathing.

I reach out and touch her face. When I feel a bit better I'll move her away from the railway line to somewhere more peaceful. Under that tree over there with the wild flowers near it.

Zelda is lying next to me too. We cling on to each other, and watch the train speed away into the distance.

'Are you alright?' I say.

'Yes,' she says. 'Are you?'

I nod. My glasses are alright too.

'We're lucky,' she says sadly.

'Yes,' I say. 'We are.'

I think about Barney and what was in his jacket pocket when I hugged him just now.

Metal syringes.

I know he won't let the others suffer any pain. He's a good dentist. He'll tell them a story about a long peaceful sleep, and it'll be a true story.

I don't know what the rest of my story will be.

It could end in a few minutes, or tomorrow, or next year, or I could be the world's most famous author in the year 1983, living in a cake shop with a dog called Jumble and my best friend Zelda.

However my story turns out, I'll never forget how lucky I am.

Barney said everybody deserves to have something good in their life at least once.

I have.

More than once.

Dear Reader,

This story came from my imagination, but it was inspired by real events.

From 1939 to 1945 the world was at war, and the leader of Germany, Adolf Hitler, tried to destroy the Jewish people in Europe. His followers, the Nazis, and those who supported them, murdered six million Jews including one and a half million children. They also killed a lot of other people, many of whom offered shelter to the Jews. We call this time of killing the Holocaust.

My grandfather was a Jew from Krakow in Poland. He left there long before that time, but his extended family didn't and most of them perished.

Ten years ago I read a book about Janusz Korczak, a Polish Jewish doctor and children's author who devoted his life to caring for young people. Over many years he helped run an orphanage for two hundred Jewish children. In 1942, when the Nazis murdered these orphans, Janusz Korczak was offered his freedom but chose to die with the children rather than abandon them.

Janusz Korczak became my hero. His story sowed a seed in my imagination.

On the way to writing this story I read many other stories – diaries, letters, notes and memories of people who were young at the time of the Holocaust.

Many of them died, but some of their stories survived, and you can find out where to read them by visiting my website or having a look at the Once *readers' notes on the* Puffin *site.*

This story is my imagination trying to grasp the unimaginable.

Their stories are the real stories.

Morris Gleitzman

www.morrisgleitzman.com
www.puffin.co.uk

Bloomsbury Grammar Guide

By the same author

On Language
Scottish Names, 1992
Good Punctuation Guide, 1992
Idioms: Their Meanings and origins, 1996

Poetry
Ayrshire Recessional, 1998

For Children
Edinburgh: A Capital Story (with Frances Jarvie), 1991
Scottish Castles, 1995
The Clans, 1995
Scotland's Vikings (with Frances Jarvie), 1997

As Editor
The Wild Ride and Other Scottish Stories, 1986
The Genius and Other Irish Stories, 1988
Scottish Folk and Fairy Tales, 1992
Irish Folk and Fairy Tales, 1992
A Friend of Humanity: Selected Stories of George Friel, 1992
The Scottish Reciter, 1993
Great Golf Stories, 1993
A Nest of Singing Birds: Nine Fettes Poets, 1995
Writing from Scotland, 1997